Patricia Scanlan was born in Dublin, where she still lives. Her books have sold worldwide and have been translated into many languages. Patricia is the series editor and a contributing author to the *Open Door* series. She also teaches creative writing to second-level students and is involved in Adult Literacy.

Find out more by visiting Patricia Scanlan on Facebook.

Also by Patricia Scanlan

Apartment 3B
Finishing Touches
Foreign Affairs
Promises, Promises
Mirror Mirror
Two for Joy
Double Wedding
Divided Loyalties

Trilogies

City Girl
City Lives
City Woman

Forgive and Forget
Happy Ever After
Love and Marriage
With All My Love

Patricia SCANLAN

Coming Home

... for Christmas

**SIMON &
SCHUSTER**

London · New York · Sydney · Toronto · New Delhi

A CBS COMPANY

First published in Great Britain by Transworld Ireland, 2009
This edition published by Simon & Schuster UK Ltd, 2014
A CBS COMPANY

1 3 5 7 9 10 8 6 4 2

Simon & Schuster UK Ltd
1st Floor
222 Gray's Inn Road
London
WC1X 8HB

www.simonandschuster.co.uk
www.simonandschuster.com.au

Simon & Schuster Australia, Sydney
Simon & Schuster India, New Delhi

A CIP catalogue record for this book is available from the British Library

ISBN Paperback 978-1-47115-456-0
ISBN eBook 978-1-47114-112-6

Typeset by Hewer Text UK Ltd, Edinburgh
Printed and bound in Great Britain by
CPI Group (UK) Ltd, Croydon CR0 4YY

To my sister, Mary, who has been by my side through thick and thin, shared my joy and sadness, minded me, encouraged me and had such fun with me. You are my rock and my best friend and this acknowledgement is long overdue! I hope you enjoy this book as much as you've enjoyed the others.

There's no future looking back.

Acknowledgements

Great tidings of comfort and joy

For all the comfort and joy I've been given in my life I give thanks, and for the gift of this book, as always, I thank Jesus, Our Lady, Mother Meera, St Joseph, St Michael, St Anthony, The Holy Spirit, White Eagle, all my Angels and Saints and Guides, and my Beloved Mother who is now with them.

When Francesca Liversidge asked for a story that would incorporate the love and warmth of family and friends to give a 'feelgood' feeling in these difficult and recessionary times, I didn't have to go far in my own life for inspiration, as I'm surrounded by so many people who give me love, cherishing and nurturing, and lots of fun to boot!

To all my Beloveds: family, friends and soulmates. How could I have written a book like this without you? A special thanks to Alil O'Shaughnessy, I owe you a loaf of currant bread! And a lot more besides.

To Sarah Lutyens who steers me along my career path with great wisdom and understanding, and who is stoic beyond measure when I begin to flap! I really do appreciate all that you, Felicity, Daisy and Jane do for me.

To Grainne Fox, my agent in the US. Thanks so much for all your energy, hard work and faith.

To Francesca Liversidge, who commissioned this book and who was such a wonderful editor for sixteen years. You were a staunch ally and a huge support in my writing career, and our friendship will last forever. Fly high and free and have lots and lots of fun with all your many friends here and over there, as only you can do.

To Linda Evans, who has taken me under her wing and has made a difficult time much less traumatic. Thank you for your kind and patient editing and your generous reassurances. Here's to new adventures.

To Jo Williamson, who deals with so many queries with such efficiency and calm assurance. I hope they know what a treasure they have in you. And to Sarah Day, my hard-working copy editor who whips the manuscript into shape. To Kate Tolley, for her good-humoured patience during our 'proofing' phone calls, and to my other proofreaders for their diligence. We authors owe you a lot!

To Nuala O'Neill, Pete Jacobs and Ian Tripp – I am only one of hundreds of authors who owe you a huge debt of gratitude. Thanks for all the work you've done on our behalf. I'll miss you all.

To Brenda Kimber, who was so kind and accommodating in her editing of *Angels of Divine Light*, an inspiring new book by my great friend, Aidan Storey. I'm sure we drove you mad but there was never even the slightest hint of irritation. Thanks so much.

To Eoin and Lauren at Transworld Ireland and to everyone in the various departments at Transworld who have given me and my novels ongoing support.

To Gill, Simon, Helen, Dec and Fergus of Gill Hess & Co for their Trojan efforts on my behalf. I couldn't wish for a better team and appreciate so much the amount of work you do for me here in Ireland. There aren't enough thanks.

*   *   *

To Billy Martin in Mullingar . . . told you I'd put you in the book! Will let you know how accurate you were, this time next year!

To Aurora Garcia in Mi Capricho who is always so kind and helpful as is Carlos. *Muchos gracias.*

And to all my very loyal readers who have supported me for all my writing career. I'm deeply grateful and appreciate all the lovely letters and compliments you give me. May all good things come into your lives. I hope you enjoy this book.

Chapter 1

A bitingly chill wind blew in off the East River and hailstones sharp as wasp stings peppered Alison Dunwoody's upraised face as she took one last look at the apartment she'd called home for the past three years. The five windows on the twelfth floor were dark now. Pitch black. No comforting glow of golden lamplight spilling out identifying it as hers, among the myriad lights that glimmered from her building.

Alison shook her head in disbelief. It wasn't her building any more. When she'd first come to New York she'd found it so strange to hear people talking about 'my building' so proprietorially. As she'd scaled the career ladder, she'd moved buildings several times, her first home being a tiny, dark studio, with

cockroaches and rattling waterpipes, in a less than salu-
brious area off Times Square; and then to a bigger
studio in Chelsea before graduating to a one-bedroom
apartment in TriBeCa. She'd lived there happily,
knowing that she was progressing well in the financial
sector. She'd studied and taken courses, the last one a
three-year course for a Chartered Wealth Management
degree, which she'd found thoroughly absorbing. After
that, she'd got a job in the private banking sector,
before leaving to join the Wealth Management team of
DJ Hamilton & Associates Financial Advisers, a prestig-
ious financial institution on Wall Street.

Her personal reward to herself, after that leap up
the ladder, was a two-bedroom apartment, uptown
between First and FDR, with a dinky balcony and a
view of the East River. Nirvana, and an affirmation of
all the gruelling hours she'd put in at her job and all
her hard work over the years.

Several of the women in her building were rich men's
mistresses. Two were first wives living in apartments
secured in divorce settlements from their ex-husbands.
One young, spoilt madam lived there thanks to her
wealthy father. Alison was paying her rent herself and
that was a source of *immense* satisfaction. True, the

kitchen in her pad was postage-stamp small and the second bedroom doubled as her office, extra closet, and repository for unironed clothes, unread magazines and anything that she needed out of sight before entertaining Jonathan Bailey, her 'current' boyfriend.

Alison chewed the inside of her lip. Jonathan, an advertising executive in his father's mega-successful TransCon Advertising Agency, was out of town at the moment. He was tying up a deal in LA and had been away for almost a month doing a root-and-branch review of the business on the west coast. Belt-tightening was essential in the current climate, he'd assured her as he spent a small fortune on a new Rolex Oyster.

When she'd told him she'd been made redundant and would have to give up her Upper East Side apartment, his tanned, handsome face had registered dismay, and she knew it wasn't because of her housing dilemma, but because he didn't want to have to offer her a place to stay. Jonathan did not like to have his wings clipped. He didn't do domesticity or exclusivity, he'd told her during their first encounter, at a cocktail party in the Hamptons at the beginning of the summer. He'd done marriage once and wouldn't be doing it again in a hurry, he'd informed her crisply.

3

'A man after my own heart,' she'd reciprocated airily. 'I can't bear to be tied down.'

'How refreshing.' Jonathan had studied her with renewed interest, and she knew she'd hooked him. With her rich auburn mane of tumbling curls, wide green eyes, and a light tan, she'd been looking particularly well that night, in an elegant, cerise sleeveless dress that showed off her well-toned body to perfection.

They'd dated casually ever since and, though she liked him, and had a good time with him, she was by no means in love with Jonathan and had no desire to move in with him. This easygoing relationship had suited Alison down to the ground. Exclusivity and domesticity were so not her scene either. Work and career advancement were her consuming passions. They made her buzz, giving her an adrenalin rush no romance had ever matched.

Alison sighed from the depths of her. She wondered how long her romance with Jonathan would last now that she was jobless and moving to a small studio no bigger than a medium-sized hotel suite. Not too long, she imagined. Part of her attraction for Jonathan was her independence, financial and otherwise. He liked that she often insisted on paying for their romantic dinners. And that she was not high maintenance. His wife was bleeding him dry, he often moaned, even though he had been born to affluence and never stinted on luxury items for himself. He was fun to be with, charming and, equally important to Alison, he knew so many movers and shakers and mixed with the crème de la crème in NY and LA. She'd been on the cusp of bringing several new clients to her firm, having met them socially with Jonathan and impressing them with her knowledge and expertise in the financial sector. It was the grace of God nothing had been firmed up and none of their wealth had been invested in Hamilton's, she thought with a shudder, remembering how quickly her world had been turned upside down.

The downturn, which had hit the financial markets with the speed of a tsunami, devastating hundreds of thousands of investors and mucking up her life big-time, was a disaster for her. She certainly wouldn't be able to pay for dinner à deux in exclusive restaurants any more, or go to Norma's, the 'in' place to have brunch in NY, on Sundays before strolling down to Central Park with the papers. She wouldn't be flying all over the country to join her boyfriend on luxury breaks in fashionable destinations. She would be counting her pennies in her tiny burrow and doing her utmost to find a new position. Jonathan would be far from impressed with her new lodgings, she thought with a wry smile, knowing what a snob he was about such things. She'd got used to the high life, got used to spending crazy money on life's little luxuries – designer shoes, bags, accessories. She'd spent $250 on a pair of Dolce & Gabbana sunglasses that time she'd gone to the Hamptons, and several hundred more on designer jeans and strappy sandals. She'd spent a fortune that weekend, including splashing out on several bottles of Krug. It hadn't cost her a thought. Now she was making a cocktail last an hour on the rare nights she went out with friends, and her fridge no longer boasted splits of champagne. In fact, her new fridge was half the size of the one she'd had in her apartment. 'Compact' was the best adjective to describe her new abode, Alison thought ruefully as she shivered in the arctic breeze.

It was a three-month sublet which she'd been lucky to acquire through her colleague and best friend, Melora, who, like her, had lost her job. Melora Buscemi had had enough of chilly New York and unemployment. She'd had to give up her loft in the Meatpacking District for the small studio off Broadway. Her BMW

Cabriolet had been repossessed and her credit card had been declined when she'd used it to pay for a new laptop when her own had crashed, with impeccable timing, the day after she became one of America's jobless. Had she still been employed, the company would have paid for a top-of-the-range model.

Melora was heading for LA for the rest of the winter, where at least she wouldn't have to pay heating bills, and the chances of finding a job had to be better than in gloomy, depressed, recession-battered New York, she reckoned somewhat illogically, the recession being nationwide. But having secured the studio for a six-month let she was reluctant to let it go, and lose her deposit.

'Look, unless Jonathan's going to pay your rent, you won't be able to manage much longer where you are without making a huge dent in what's left of your savings. Why don't you sublet your apartment and take my little pad until you get sorted?' Melora offered kindly as they sat sipping cocktails in Chez Toni's, a club they'd had to queue forty minutes to gain entrance to. They'd watched glumly from behind the cordon as the Town Cars and sleek limos deposited gorgeous women in barely there designer dresses and skyscraper heels, and cool Armani- and Gucci-clad guys – the kind Melora was desperate to meet – swanned in to be cocooned in the rarefied, roped-off, security-guarded areas, where they could drink champagne untroubled by lesser beings who had to queue.

Had Jonathan been with them they wouldn't have had to do anything so déclassé as queue. He was one of the social elite who had that magical access to clubs and restaurants, and swanky airport lounges. Jonathan never, ever turned right on an aircraft, and the few times she'd travelled with him, neither had Alison. Now it all seemed like a dream.

'Or even better, honey,' her friend interrupted her musings, 'why don't you come to LA with me? We could rent a place together and wow the corporate heads with our mega-impressive CVs, stunning good looks and, like, totally sophisticated NY cool.' Melora grinned, showing her strong, white teeth. With smooth ebony skin and a long-limbed, curvy body, she looked ten years younger than her thirty-five years. 'I suppose you wouldn't want to leave Jonathan?' She arched a perfectly shaped eyebrow.

'It's not that, Mel,' Alison sighed. 'I can't see me and Jonathan lasting much longer, to be honest. He doesn't do "failure", and once he sees me in a walk-up studio that my bed wouldn't even fit in, he's going to think, "Loser".'

'Don't say that, you're not a loser. This is un-precedented – it's a recession. It's got nothing to do with our lack of skills or job performance,' Mel protested indignantly.

'Well, I ain't a winner right now.' Alison grimaced. 'Heading for mid-thirties, jobless, almost homeless, living on my savings, which are dwindling much faster than I'd like – after nearly fifteen years of work-ing my ass off, I haven't got much to show for it. My investments got such a hammering, and my bonuses were in company shares and they're down the Swannee just like yours.'

'You can add "manless" to that list for me,' Melora remarked gloomily.

'I'm going to be manless too, soon. You can bet on it.' Alison shrugged.

'And it doesn't even bother you, girl. You and I are so different in that regard. I want the man! I want the kids! I want the home!' Melora eyed a hot guy who was strolling past with two splits of champagne.

'My sister Olivia has all that. I'd go crazy – I'd feel

so smothered and claustrophobic. Uuggghh!' Alison winced at the notion.

'You just haven't met the right man yet. I'm telling you, when you meet him you'll know, and we'll see how claustrophobic you feel *then*.'

'Dream on,' grinned Alison.

'Girl, we lived a high ol' life though here in New York City.' Mel chuckled. 'And you can't deny that. Come to LA with me. Let's give it a whirl?' she urged.

'I don't know, I don't like LA. All that body- beautiful stuff, all that lettuce-leaf lifestyle, all that phoney posturing and posing and edginess and the way people are so busy looking over your shoulder when they're talking to you . . . scouting . . . No thanks. I'm too old for it – and I hate constant sunshine: it would drive me crazy.'

'How can you say that, you mad Irishwoman you? That holiday I spent with you in Ireland where it rained non-stop and you said you didn't mind it. You're crazy *already*,' her friend teased, raising her cocktail glass to her.

'Anyway, talking of home, it's my mam's seventieth birthday. I'm going home next week, don't forget. I think I might even stay an extra ten days for Christmas; it would make her so happy. She doesn't even know I'm coming home for her birthday. I can't believe she's seventy.' Alison took a slug of her drink, wishing she could get hammered, but alcohol was having no effect on her mood tonight.

'Completely forgot about that. So I guess we won't be seeing each other for a while,' Melora said sadly.

'Don't say that,' Alison protested miserably.

'Have you told them at home about work?' Melora drained her cocktail.

'Nope. Although, in fairness, my mam would say something like "Let it go, the Universe will provide, when one door closes another door opens if you let it." She has a great outlook on life in that regard. My dad would worry a lot more. But it would still upset them, and I don't want to ruin the party and Christmas. Have you told yours?'

'Naw, it would only worry them too. And my dad's not been well. They don't need an unemployed daughter to be concerned about. They'll want me to come home and, honey, I just couldn't face a cold Chicago winter living back with my folks – even though I love them,' she added hastily.

'I know, it would be like taking a backward step, going back to your childhood almost. I'm not going to say a word. I'll just let on everything's fine.' Alison frowned as she pronged an olive and chewed it.

'Things will work out for us both,' Melora said stoutly.

'Sure,' agreed Alison heartily. 'We'll be fine. Just fine.'

Three days later, her best friend had jetted off to LA relieved at least that Alison was subletting her studio.

Tears slid down Alison's cheeks as she remembered their night out and their upbeat talk. Things were far from fine, she reflected, as the hailstones continued their onslaught. Her own apartment was awaiting a new tenant. She'd pulled in every contact she had, targeted dozens of firms, even cold-called executives to try and sell herself and get a job, but recession was embedded and firms were being inundated with applications from high performers who'd lost their jobs in the financial and economic meltdown. And so far, five weeks down the line from the day she'd arrived at her Wall Street office to discover that the owner and CEO of her company had drunk a bottle of whiskey, swallowed a fistful of sleepers and died in the early hours of the morning – she hadn't had a whisper of a job.

Daniel J. Hamilton, charismatic CEO and founder of Hamilton & Associates, had taken a hit when Lehman

Bros. had collapsed, but he'd restructured the company's finances, tightened up their operation and kept going, until the news had filtered along Wall Street that another disaster with highly respected financier Bernie Madoff was on the cards – far more damaging than the Lehman debacle. Hamilton, over-extended as he was, knew he couldn't claw his way out of this second catastrophe. He was an honourable man who had always dealt with his clientele with the height of professional integrity. He could not face telling his many clients, some high profile, his employees, and his family that they had lost fortunes because of the investment advice his firm had given in good faith, investments he'd believed in and invested in himself, investments he'd urged his employees to put their bonuses in. He'd locked himself in his office with a bottle of Jack Daniels and the sleeping tablets his doctor had prescribed for him the previous month, written a note to his wife and children and become another victim of unscrupulous, unprincipled men who thought they were above the law.

Alison and Melora, along with the other dazed employees, had been told by the financial director that their jobs were gone, the business was bankrupt, the receivers were being called in and they should collect their belongings and go home. Alison had gone from being a highly regarded senior vice-president with a very affluent lifestyle to being jobless and, it seemed, unemployable, in the blink of an eye. And she wasn't alone or the worst off by far. She'd seen grown men cry at the thought of having to go home and tell their wives and children they had no job and would no longer be able to pay their mortgages, college fees and health-care bills. She'd seen the fear in their faces as all their security had been pulled from under them in the space of a ten-minute speech. People like them – highly educated, highly qualified professionals – didn't get made redundant. This was America, the land of milk and honey, the land of golden opportunity. The shock and disbelief were palpable. The TV cameras had filmed them leaving the offices, and they'd been on all the news channels for a day or two and then it had been someone else's turn.

Now, here she was standing on the pavement, about to hail a taxi to take her to a cramped little walk-up, most of her possessions in storage, and she felt lonely, scared and oppressed. Strange, unfamiliar emotions that rattled her confidence and brought her to the edge of panic. What was she going to do if she couldn't get a job? How long could she last without an income?

There were jobs in Hong Kong, Singapore, and other foreign destinations – she'd scoured the internet looking at the positions on offer – but the idea of uprooting to another country and starting afresh was unnerving and not one that she relished. She'd done all that when she was younger. Now it didn't seem as exciting a prospect. Her mother might well say that the Universe would provide, and it looked as though Alison was going to have to put the theory to the test, even though she didn't want to. Trusting in providence was not her forte, she thought wryly. She liked to be in control.

Suddenly, although she'd been dreading the thought of going home to Port Ross, Alison wanted to be there more than anything. Wanted to feel her mother's warm, loving hug and listen to her words of wisdom, and inhale the familiar woody scent of her father's pipe, knowing that there was one place at least that she would be welcomed with open arms. Port Ross, the small fishing village on the north-east coast of Ireland just thirty miles from Dublin where she'd grown up, seemed far more inviting than the bitterly cold, noisy, grimy, bustling city street she was standing on.

Her parents lived in a homely dormer bungalow right on top of a cliff at the sea's edge. The sound of the sea caressing the beach had lullabied her to sleep every night, and the orange gold of the sunrise painting the sea and sky had woken her each morning, along with the smell of her mother's homemade brown bread and scones wafting up the stairs.

Her older sister, Olivia, still lived in the village, with her husband and three little girls. They'd be fast asleep now, after a supper of hot chocolate and buttery toast in front of the fire, a tradition Olivia had carried on from their own childhood. God, she'd love to be sitting in front of a real fire, watching it roaring up the chimney, listening to the crackling song of the wood as it blazed merrily, sipping creamy hot chocolate and eating toast dripping with melting butter and jam, Alison thought longingly.

Impulsively, she pulled out her cell phone. It was night time at home, but Olivia would get the message in the morning Alison thought, hailing a taxi that had its light on. She gave the midtown address and settled back against the seat, her fingers flying over the keys.

Hi O. How U? How are the plans for the surprise party going? Can't wait 2 C every 1. So glad I'm coming home. A xx

Chapter 2

'Do you see her now? She can't walk in those high heels, and that one there, she's flat-footed.'

Holy Mother!, Olivia Hammond thought in dismay as she gave her elderly uncle a dig in the ribs. 'Shush, they'll hear you,' she hissed, noting the amused glance of one of the nurses hurrying past them along the busy hospital corridor where they were sitting.

'Not a'tall, girl, wasn't I whisperin'?' Leo Dunwoody declared indignantly as he sat beside her, his arms folded, taking a great interest in all that was going on around him.

'Do you see the one in the pink- and blue-striped top over there? She'd be one of the lower orders; she wouldn't be a real nurse now,' Leo observed knowingly. Although he thought he was whispering, the people on either side of them could hear him.

'Mr Dunwoody, we'll take you now.' A 'real' nurse popped her head out of the Breathing Test Room opposite them, and Olivia watched with fond exasperation as the elderly man stood up and made his way into the room with a cheery wave of his walking stick.

'Right, lassie, we'd better get on with it, I suppose,' he boomed as the door closed behind him. Olivia exhaled a long, deep breath and stretched her legs in front of her. The plastic chairs were uncomfortable, and they'd been there for the past three-quarters of an hour. The appointment was for eleven, but Uncle Leo preferred to be early wherever he was going. That was all very well, but Olivia was pushed for time. She'd taken flexi-time to bring him to his appointment, time she could ill afford. She job-shared in the administration department of a busy third-level-education college, and exam time was always hectic.

There was a hot-drinks machine further along the corridor, and she walked to it, rooted in her bag for some loose coins, dropped them into the slot and selected a cappuccino. She'd only taken a few gulps from her coffee at breakfast time, between trying to get lunch boxes ready and dealing with the trauma of her youngest daughter, Ellie, dropping her baby tooth into the cat's food dish and the twins having a row about their Nintendos while she was out the back hanging out the clothes which probably wouldn't dry anyway in the cold. And it looked like rain, she thought gloomily. She sipped her cappuccino and tried to suppress a yawn as her phone rang. Her mother's number flashed up on the screen.

'Hello, love, how did Leo get on? It was so kind of you to offer to take him.' Esther Dunwoody's voice floated down the line.

'Hi, Mam, we're still here. They were late and we were here three-quarters of an hour beforehand – you know Leo,' Olivia moaned.

'Ah, God love you,' Esther sympathized.

'And not only that – you know the way he's deaf and he thinks he's whispering and the things he's saying. My nerves are shot wondering what he's going to come out with next. He told me this morning I could do with getting my hair cut, I was looking a bit like a scarecrow.'

Esther chuckled. 'He's himself. Tact was never his greatest quality. Anyway, I was just ringing to say don't bother cooking dinner for yourself and the girls, I'll put your name in the pot, and why don't you tell Michael to come straight from work—'

'He was coming anyway. He wants to lick the wooden spoon when you're making the puddings. He's worse than the girls – they're so excited.' Olivia grinned.

'Honest to goodness, Livvy, I've never been this late making the puddings, I'm getting old. I'm going to buy them next year.' Her mother sighed. 'I forgot to get eggs. Will you get me a dozen? I want to make a small cake for Leo later in the week while I'm at it. I know he's partial to Christmas cake.'

'You're a big softie, Mam. I'll see you in a while,' Olivia said, delighted with her mother's offer. Not having to cook dinner would be a great help. She needed to make a start on tidying up the spare room for her younger sister's arrival. There was a mountain of ironing that needed tending, and she was anxious to get a move on wrapping the Christmas presents that lay at the end of the bed, and one that needed changing before Alison came home for their mother's surprise party.

There was so much to do, and she hadn't even thought of writing a Christmas card. Leo had remarked when she'd collected him this morning that he hadn't got hers and Michael's yet. She'd try to get down to them tonight, she promised herself. The mail sign on her phone was flashing, and she knew her inbox was full. She might as well do a bit of deleting while she was waiting and put her time to good use.

Her fingers raced over the keys, and when she'd deleted her sent items and half a dozen messages in her inbox, three messages gunned back in rapid succession. One was from her sister. Olivia opened it, noting that it had been sent the previous day. She really should delete her messages more often, she thought, as she read it.

Hi O. How U? How are the plans for the surprise party going? Can't wait 2 C every 1. So glad I'm coming home. A xx

Olivia frowned. Bully for you! she thought crossly. Nice for Alison to breeze in from New York like the homecoming queen, be made a fuss of at the party she hadn't had to lift a finger to organize, and then breeze out because she couldn't take time off work to spend Christmas with her family. No fear of her being at home to bring their uncle to the chest clinic, or help out with the cooking and shopping when both their parents had been felled by a particularly nasty flu a couple of weeks ago. Alison was too busy acting like a character out of *Sex and the City* to give a hoot about what was going on in boring old Port Ross.

Olivia scowled as she deleted her sister's text. Alison had demurred at first about coming home to celebrate her mother's seventieth. Did she not know how lucky she was to have a mother as good as Esther? She wouldn't always be with them; significant birthdays *should* be celebrated, Olivia had pointed out a touch sharply when the discussion had taken place over the phone earlier in the year. Her younger sister wouldn't think twice of flying to Hawaii or LA for R&R. She could damn well get her ass in gear and come home for her mother, Olivia had insisted, annoyed that she'd had to push her sister to come to such an important family event.

'OK, OK, I was hoping to bring her and Dad over for a few days. They always enjoy their trips to New York,' Alison had argued, clearly irritated at Olivia doing her bossy older sister act.

'That would be fine if it was an ordinary birthday, but seventy is an important birthday, and we need to mark it in a special way with all the family,' Olivia declared, frustrated that she had to point out the obvious.

Alison had agreed after that and, being her generous self, offered to pay half the cost. That was one thing Olivia couldn't fault her sister on: she was generous to a fault with her money, even if she was less than giving with her time. What a charmed life Alison led, with only herself to worry about. She worked hard, but she played hard too, and her free time was hers to do with entirely as she wished.

Olivia hadn't enjoyed free time in years. Three young children, elderly relatives, a busy husband, a household to run and her own job left her constantly chasing her tail. She was lucky to get a read of *Hello!* in the bath, she thought ruefully, remembering some of the descriptive emails her sister had sent while skiing, or scuba-diving, or meeting wealthy hunks at parties in the Hamptons.

Olivia had flown out to stay with Alison for long weekends several times over the past few years because Michael, her husband, had insisted she needed a break. The difference in their lifestyles always fascinated Olivia. There was absolutely no comparison and, if the truth were told, she felt her life was deadly boring in contrast, and she always came home unsettled and dissatisfied, knowing that she was hurtling towards forty and middle age. It would take her a month or so to get into her routine and settled down and to regain some sort of equilibrium.

Although, in fairness, she reminded herself as she sat impatiently waiting for Leo, when she'd arrived home after the last visit and her three little girls had hurled themselves into her arms at the airport and Michael had stood, thumbs hooked into his jeans and a big smile on his face, she'd felt an unexpected surge of happiness, which was enhanced even more when her mother hugged her tightly and said, 'I'm so glad you're home, love. I missed you terribly, even though you were only gone for a few days.' Olivia smiled at the memory. She and Esther had a very close bond, and it was her dearest wish that her own daughters would have as close a bond with her when they were adults.

'Well, I'm gaspin' after that. Bring me home like a good girl and make me a nice cup of tea.' Uncle Leo limped over to her, red-cheeked, white hair sticking up, wheezing like a train. 'Or would you like to get

me one of those Snack Box things? I'm hungry too.'
He flopped down wearily on the chair beside her,
puffing and panting. 'They gave me a right going-
over in there. I'm banjaxed. You must be hungry too
after all that waiting. I'll treat you to a chippie, and I
want to buy a few sweets for the girls.'

Olivia's heart sank. Friday was the worst day for the
queues in the chipper, and the precious window she'd
been carving for herself to get the spare room sorted
before the girls got home from school was rapidly
dwindling away.

'And do you know what I want you to get me? I
want you to get me a nice pair of gloves for your
mother, and a pair for your da – and would the girls
wear gloves? It's been a fierce cold winter and I want
something useful for them for under the Christmas
tree. I could put twenty euros each down a finger for
them.' Leo looked at her enquiringly, his blue eyes,
bright and lively, belying his eighty-two years. Her
heart softened. He loved the girls and took a great
interest in the tapestry of their lives, and they loved
him as much as they loved their grandparents.
Childless, his wife Kitty had died ten years
previously.

'Gloves would be great,' she said kindly, taking his arm to walk down the corridor.

'I'd say that lady's up from the country. See, she has her case with her. Probably an overnight job,' he commented in a fairly stentorian tone, raising his hat to an elderly woman sitting on one of the chairs. The woman caught Olivia's exasperated gaze and smiled back.

'Come on, Uncle Leo, let's go get a Snack Box.' Olivia sighed, remembering she had to stop at the shops and get a dozen eggs for her mother while she was at it. She was going to have to try and get her uncle's Christmas shopping done, and she needed to order the flowers and cake for the surprise party. The sooner Alison was home the better: she could sort out the flowers and decorate the private room Olivia had booked in the Golden Dragon, the popular Chinese restaurant on the Dublin road, a mile or so out of the village.

Esther loved having a meal there, and she and Olivia would try and eat out there every six weeks or so. Her mother wasn't expecting a birthday bash. As far as she knew, they were having a meal out in the restaurant with the girls. She had no idea that Alison was coming home. *That* would be the best surprise of all for her, thought Olivia, and her sister didn't even appreciate the fact. Sometimes Olivia felt like the prodigal son's brother, the one who was taken very much for granted and never had a fatted calf cooked in his honour despite all his good work.

Oh, get over yourself! She scowled, annoyed at her childishness, then linked her uncle's arm in hers and was rewarded with an appreciative pat on the hand.

'You're a good niece, Olivia, and I'm grateful to you for your kindness. You take after your mother in that regard. I just want you to know that,' Leo said appreciatively, leaning on her more than he usually did. The tests had taken it out of him today, she noted as they walked slowly down the steps of the hospital.

'Thanks, Uncle Leo, you're welcome. Now let's get you home and feed you before I collect the girls from school, and you can go and have a good nap for yourself afterwards,' she said affectionately.

One thing about her uncle, he appreciated what she and Esther did for him, and that made all the difference. Some of her friends had relatives who were utterly demanding and thoroughly selfish.

27

She'd get the spare room sorted one way or another – it wasn't the Queen coming to stay, it was only her sister; and it was only for one night, because her parents would want Alison to stay with them for the couple of days she was home. Another thought struck her: Alison would probably expect her to be at the airport. It would be a bit callous to expect her to get a taxi, she supposed. That was if she *could* get a taxi, she thought grimly. A friend of hers had missed a flight to Spain because the taxi men had gone on strike with little or no warning – you couldn't depend on them these days. Besides, it was always nice to be met by family, especially after a transatlantic flight. It would be different if she was jetting over from London or Europe.

She hadn't factored that in at all. Damn. She'd think about it later: right now she had to get Leo sorted, do her mother's shopping and get the girls picked up from school. There weren't enough hours in the day, Olivia fretted silently, helping her uncle into the car and mentally ticking one chore off her list for today.

Chapter 3

Esther Dunwoody lined a baking tray with grease-proof paper and emptied several packets of sultanas and muscatel raisins on to it. She slid the tray into the oven to heat the fruit so that it would swell nicely for the pudding mix.

She'd been making or helping to make Christmas puddings for a long time now – nearly *sixty-five* years, she thought with a stomach-lurching shock, remembering back to the fire-warmed kitchen in her parents' house. It had a pantry just off it, where her mother stored all her baking ingredients. As a child she'd loved that pantry, loved the smell of her mother's homemade brown soda loaves and currant breads. There was either a rich tea brack, apple or rhubarb tart, a jam sponge or a tray of fairy cakes on the cake shelf, and always, her absolute favourites, scones, that would be served with homemade blackberry jam and, as an extra treat on Sundays, a big dollop of cream. Although she'd been baking for years and got many compliments, Esther never felt that she had *quite* the light touch her own mother had had.

She could still remember as a five-year-old standing on the little stool beside her mother, sister and brother and cutting cherries in half and tipping a plate full of sultanas and raisins into the big pot where her mother stirred the mixture. Then the most special moment, when they all queued up to make a wish.

It really was a cycle, she mused as she shook two cartons of red cherries on to a plate and licked the sticky sugar coating off her fingers. She had taken Olivia and Alison to do the Christmas baking at her mother's house during the years of their childhood, and her young daughters had loved the excitement of it all. Now Olivia was bringing her three little girls to stand around the kitchen table to slice and stir and mix and taste and make their wishes, just as she and her siblings had all those years ago. And the same sense of excitement and anticipation would fill the kitchen as mothers and daughters weighed and poured and sieved and whisked, using the Christmas-pudding recipe that had passed down through several genera-tions of Esther's family.

Esther wiped her hands and went to the drawer that housed her collection of floral aprons. She picked out four and laid them on the big wooden table behind her. Part of the excitement for her grand-daughters was wearing an apron. It was almost a badge of honour, Esther thought with a smile, looking forward to the afternoon with her precious brood. She loved the anticipation of Christmas. The happiest time of her life had been when her parents were still alive and she and her husband, Liam, and Olivia and Alison had celebrated the festive season together, cooking and decorating and Christmas shopping and going to Mass *en famille* on Christmas morning.

And now her daughters were grown women, and Olivia had children of her own, and Alison . . . Alison hadn't been home for Christmas in three years. Esther felt a stab of sadness. Her daughter worked hard in New York. She came home for a week every summer, but she couldn't afford the time off at Christmas, and Esther always felt a terrible ache of loneliness at Mass and at the dinner table, despite the clamour of the girls with their excited little faces. Liam always knew what she was feeling, and he'd whisper, 'Maybe next year she'll make it.'

Would it be different if Alison was married and had children of her own? Esther wondered. Would that strengthen the ties of family, ties that her youngest daughter had always felt so oppressively binding?

Olivia and Alison were chalk and cheese. Olivia was the typical older daughter, with a sense of filial responsibility which free-spirited Alison had never been encumbered with. Alison had shaken the dust of Port Ross from her high-heel-shod feet as soon as she could, embracing city life with gusto. She'd worked hard in college and travelled the world before finally settling in New York, where she'd spent three years studying for a degree at night. New York was the city for her; there was no denying that. The buzz, vibrancy and opportunities to succeed suited her daughter's ambitious nature down to the ground.

She and Liam had visited her in New York several times over the past few years and thoroughly enjoyed every second of their trips. Since the girls had grown up and left home, she and her husband had spent holidays in the Far East and the Gulf, and had the trip of a lifetime to visit her brother in Melbourne. They'd taken weekend breaks in European cities and explored the wide variety of cultures on offer, but Esther's favourite city was New York.

She envied Alison the opportunities she had. Modern women had so many options that hadn't been available to her generation. Esther had had to give up her job once she'd married Liam and become pregnant. There were no crèches back then. Women were expected to stay at home and mind their children. That had been hard, because Esther had always had a strong streak of independence, which she'd had to surrender to being a wife and mother. Giving up her own salary had been a sacrifice. Giving up her job as a staff officer in the Civil Service because of the 'marriage bar' had been even worse. Women had been treated badly in those unenlightened days, but looking at how stressed Olivia was, trying to juggle career and family, Esther could see the other side of the coin. Olivia was 'time poor', as they described it now. Not for her the luxury of spending a morning playing with her children on the beach and then having a picnic just because the sun was shining. Not for her the freedom to take a bus into town once the children were safely in school, to shop at leisure or stroll around an art gallery or museum soaking up the fruits of others' creativity. Neither had Esther had to worry about the expense of a big mortgage and two cars, as Olivia had to. Sometimes Esther felt her elder daughter would like to give up her job and be a stay-at-home mother, just to get off the treadmill of her hectic life for a while.

Alison's life was so different and one that Esther would love to have experienced. How wonderful to have no one but yourself to worry about, how liberating to be able to take off at the drop of a hat to go skiing in Colorado, or diving in the Caribbean, or windsurfing in Hawaii, as Alison had in the past few years. How delightful to be able to spend an entire Saturday wandering from exhibition to exhibition in the Met, Esther's favourite New York haunt.

Alison was privileged indeed, but she worked hard for it. She was at her desk by seven thirty, having first done a workout at the gym. She didn't seem to miss home at all, and Esther felt sad sometimes that the daughter who had been so lovingly reared had let go of them all so easily.

Still, she had Olivia and her little girls, she comforted herself as she lined up brown sugar, cinnamon, allspice, nutmeg, almond essence, lemons and a bottle of whiskey. Ellie, Kate and Lia were the joy of her life, and if Alison, by some miracle, were to settle down at home and marry and have children, she would be *perfectly* happy, Esther decided, setting aside her pudding ingredients and starting to cut steak into cubes and flouring them to braise. She'd add stock and seasoning and diced carrots and turnips to the pot, to simmer slowly on the hob.

It was a freezing-cold day; a chill easterly blew in off the choppy gunmetal sea. Esther could see the whitecaps pounding against the rocks across the field at Smuggler's Cove. The trees swayed, their branches long grey skeleton fingers in the wind.

The girls would need something warm and nourishing after their tiring day at school. She could heat the braised steak for Michael, her son-in-law, when he came home from work, and she'd give him an extra helping of her creamy mustard mash, his favourite. He was exactly like Liam in that regard, a real meat, potato and veg man.

'Are these enough for you?' Her husband came through the kitchen door with a big basin of breadcrumbs that he'd grated from half a dozen batch loaves.

'Perfect.' She smiled at him. 'I suppose I should buy the ready-crumbed ones, but I don't think they'd give the puddings the same substance. Batch bread is the best, I think.'

'Well, the girls always thought so. Remember the way they used to pick at the loaves? And Ellie, Lia and Kate were doing exactly the same thing yesterday. It brought me back, looking at them.' Liam put the breadcrumbs down and snaffled a cherry.

'I'm glad we're passing on the old traditions, and that we haven't succumbed to modernity,' Esther remarked. 'Even if you're the one who had to grate them.'

'It wouldn't be the same opening a bag of bread-crumbs,' her husband agreed.

'Mind, I was tempted to buy them this year, I was even tempted to buy a pudding – that dose of flu knocked the stuffing out of me,' Esther confessed, as she washed and wiped her hands and turned to face her beloved.

'I know, I'm still wheezing,' Liam said gloomily. 'We're getting old, pet, and I don't like it, not one bit.'

'Me neither . . . imagine – I'll be seventy! I just can't believe it.' She shook her head, still shocked at the notion.

'Well, you don't look it,' Liam said gallantly.

'Do I not, even though I stopped dyeing my hair?' She arched an eyebrow at him.

'Not at all,' he said, caressing her silky silver bob. 'And you certainly don't act it,' he added teasingly, blue eyes twinkling as he brushed a streak of flour off her cheek. 'And you'll be the same age as me, and I'm still a young fella at heart.'

'We did well, didn't we? We reared the girls the best we could, we have the grandchildren to spoil, we don't owe a penny to anyone . . . and . . . most importantly . . .' she slipped her arms around his waist '. . . we still love each other, don't we?'

'Ummm.' Liam rested his chin on her head as he drew her close.

'Is that a yes or a no?'

'Oh, for goodness' sake, woman, do we have to get into all that mushy stuff?' He groaned in exasperation.

'That mushy stuff is very important, mister.'

'We've been married for forty-five years – isn't that enough for you?'

'No, dear, it isn't. It's nice to hear the words "I love you" every now and again,' Esther retorted. Even after all these years, her husband still found it difficult to express his love in words.

Liam took a deep breath. 'I love you, Esther, will that do you?' he said gruffly.

'There, that wasn't so hard, now was it?' She grinned at him, raising her face for a kiss as their arms tightened around each other.

Chapter 4

Alison pulled the duvet over her head to try and shut out the sound of the rackety waterpipes gurgling and rattling overhead as the tenant upstairs took a shower. She should get up and go to the gym, she supposed; her fee was paid up until the end of December. At least it would give her something to do. But it was dark and freezing cold, and she could see a drift of snow piled up on the windowsill. Blizzards had been forecast for the weekend, and the wind chill was sending icy tentacles into the building. Every time the front door opened as the various inhabitants left for work, freezing gusts wafted up the stairs to her first-floor landing and wove under her door. Melora should have gone higher up, Alison thought gloomily. There was a third-floor apartment for rent in the same building, but who would want to lug everything up flights of stairs? 157 Dayton Street did not boast an elevator.

Alison snuggled into the warm hollow in the unfamiliar bed. She had slept badly in her new, strange surroundings, and she couldn't face getting up to start cold-calling investment firms in the soul-destroying search for a job. Her eyes drooped. She'd been unable to sleep on the soft mattress. She'd have to buy an orthopaedic one, and to hell with the cost. A good night's sleep was imperative if she was to keep sharp and focused and on top of her game. She'd lain in the dark, unwilling to switch on her lamp, not wanting to see the stacks of boxes that needed unpacking. The two friends who had helped her move were planning to come at the weekend to help her settle in. 'Settle' was the appropriate word. How could this nightmare be happening?

This was the proverbial land of opportunity where hard work was lauded and getting to the top was within everyone's grasp. Obama had proved that for sure. Jobs had been a dime a dozen when she'd arrived in America, eight years ago. Now, in the banking and financial sector, there wasn't one to be had. What the hell was she going to do? She couldn't stay living in Manhattan unless she had a salary coming in. She had money tied up in a bond but she was reluctant to cash it in early; because she'd take a hit, it was down 15 per cent. Her shares in the company were worthless. Shares she'd had in Anglo at home were down the tubes because of the mismanagement of the bank by avaricious bankers, and the AIB and BOI ones she had were on the floor.

She'd never felt so unnerved before, never felt such knots of anxiety and, even worse, fear, in her stomach. It was demoralizing and unsettling, and for the first time in her life she felt totally out of control. The professional in her knew it would take time before the US economy began its recovery; the human part hoped against hope that a miracle would happen quickly, especially now that Obama was in charge and there was talk of 'green shoots of recovery' on Wall Street.

A sudden urge to ring her parents almost overwhelmed her. She wanted to hear Esther tell her the news from home and hear her dad's gravelly voice, strong and reassuring. What a relief it would be to tell them her sorry saga. But she couldn't do that, not before her mother's surprise party. It would ruin it for her, and Alison wouldn't do that in a million years. Her heart sank as she remembered that she'd assured Olivia that she'd pay half the cost of the party and half the cost of the bangle she'd bought in Tiffany's on her credit card. She'd paid for her flight home months ago, a premium ticket – that hadn't cost her a thought. She should make the most of it; she wouldn't be flying premium again for a long time, the way things were going. It would be back to economy for her. *That* was a painful realization. It made her feel like a failure. She'd worked so hard for her luxuries; they hadn't been handed to her on a plate like Jonathan's had.

He'd phoned her to see how she was getting on. She could hear women laughing in the background. He was at his friend's house in Malibu, and they were all having brunch. If she wanted, he could ask his friend, a risk manager in a Californian financial institution, to keep an eye out for an opening for her, he offered magnanimously. If she got a job on the west coast, she'd only see him when he flew out on business every month or thereabouts. So much for their great romance, she thought in wry amusement. 'Do that,' she'd told him. 'And don't forget Melora, she's out in LA too.' If a job came up out there, she'd think about it if all else failed.

Alison yawned and stretched lethargically. Usually she slept like a log, but last night she'd twisted and turned until desperation had got the better of her. She'd got out of bed and gone to the little galley kitchen and poured herself a stiff brandy and port, hoping that turning to drink in the middle of a sleepless night wasn't the first step to alcoholism. She'd padded back to bed and propped herself up against the Egyptian-cotton-clad pillows she'd brought with her, flicked through the TV channels and spent an hour watching *My Super Sweet Sixteen Party*, aghast at the obnoxious, spoilt teenagers trying to outdo their friends with lavish parties. Three of them had received cars from their parents – and not just run-of-the-mill cars: one had got a Merc, another a Range Rover, another a Lexus. Another one had had the designer of the clothes Nicole Kidman wore for *Moulin Rouge* design a replica of a dress for her. And had got a video message from the actress, as her impressed friends had stood with their mouths open. Alison had sat watching with *her* mouth open. What on earth was she doing watching such rubbish? This had to be her lowest point ever. It stung to think those kids had cars she couldn't afford to drive now. She was an unemployed thirty-two-year-old professional who'd worked her butt off, and sixteen-year-old kids out there were swanning around in Mercs!

It was crazy, irresponsible stuff. What sort of values did those precocious teens have? None. Wealth could be so corrupting, she'd seen that herself. Seen how people had borrowed more and more to buy stocks and shares from banks which had been eager to lend, ignoring the fact that their clients were gambling on making a profit with loans way beyond their means. The whole pack of cards had come tumbling down, and while she'd lost out on her job, and her bonuses and shares, at least she still had *some* values, she'd reflected, turning off the TV and eventually falling into a restless sleep, until the sound of the gurgling waterpipes had woken her up.

I think I'll just lie here for a little while longer, she thought as she heard the front door close again, and her eyes drooped and she fell fast asleep, the first time ever she'd had a lie-in on a working day during all her time in New York.

It was after eleven when she woke, bleary-eyed and ravenously hungry. She stared around her, wondering where the hell was she, before the stomach-dropping realization hit. Alison slumped back against her pillows and gazed around. To her right, a long narrow sash window looked out on to the grey cement wall of the building next door. She hadn't even bothered to pull down the cream blind, figuring that no one could see her on the first floor. A cream chest of drawers stood underneath the window. To her left was a bedside locker with a lamp and, at right angles to the locker, a closet that would have to hold not only her clothes but also her shoes, her collection of designer handbags, accessories and sports gear. An ottoman sat at the end of her bed for her bedlinen, and to use as extra seating. An archway led into a sitting room which had another, bigger sash window facing her bed; beneath it a small desk with a reading lamp on it. Along the wall stood some bookshelves. A purple sofa and an armchair faced a plasma TV. A narrow hallway led to the tiny galley kitchen, bathroom and the front door which opened out on to the landing, off which were two other studios.

As studios went, it wasn't bad. The sage-green walls had a soothing ambiance; the blinds and curtains were relatively new and clean; the cream-painted window-sills and doors toned nicely with the green; and the cooker and fridge in the kitchen were new. The building had been recently renovated, Melora had told Alison, and, indeed, the rooms were freshly painted, as were the hallway and landings. Had she found it when she'd first started work in Manhattan she'd have been thrilled with it – it was far, far superior to the dark little dump she'd first lived in – but she'd evolved way beyond a studio, however well maintained, in a not very upmarket area off Broadway. This was a major-league retrograde step, in her opinion.

Alison slid out of bed and walked over to the window at the front of the building, which looked out over a grey, slush-covered street with buildings similar to her own. Grey seemed to be the predominant colour, all depressing and lacking in character. She could see a drug store, coffee shop and deli and liquor store across the street. Further along, a barber's, a hair salon, a laundromat and a small grocery store gave splashes of colour with their signage and shop fronts. Melora had picked well: all the basic amenities were right at her doorstep, and Alison tried to see the positive in her own situation.

On the other hand, bags of refuse had been put out for collection, and a scrawny dog sniffed around one of them, pawing it until the contents spread on to the roadway. A few emaciated trees, thin branches bowed disconsolately under the unwelcome weight of snow, lined either side of the street. There was nothing of the cosmopolitan, smart, uptown atmosphere of her old address, just a general air of shabby greyness. The rumble of the subway trains broke the silence every so often, and the noise of the traffic inching along, muffled somewhat by the snow that was flying down in huge white flakes, blotting out the dreary sky.

Alison gave a sigh that came from her toes. She needed to get in some provisions, and she needed coffee badly. She'd throw on a pair of jeans and a warm woollen jumper and parka and head across to the coffee shop for breakfast. After that she would make a plan for the day. How strange it was not to have every hour of her day accounted for, but strangely liberating, she decided as she rummaged in a big brown box that held some clothes and found a black rollneck jumper. Another box held her jeans and another her underwear. Just as well she'd taken the precaution of labelling them as the packers had filled them.

It didn't take long to dress. She couldn't face showering, and she barely covered her face with a dusting of shimmer powder, a far cry from the full make-up she applied every morning before going to work. She didn't care; she was hardly going to meet anyone she needed to impress today. Not wearing make-up made her feel like she was on holidays, she thought a little wildly, tracing on some lipgloss to protect her lips from the cold.

After breakfast she'd phone home. It would be afternoon there and it would be comforting to hear familiar and loving voices, Alison thought as she wrapped a scarf around her neck, pulled a hat down over her auburn hair, slipped her hands into soft leather gloves and headed out of her apartment.

Ten minutes later she was nibbling on a muffin and sipping scalding-hot, strong black coffee. It was good coffee, she had to admit as she gazed around her. The red Formica table had coffee rings which the waitress's perfunctory wipe with a dingy brown cloth hadn't made any impression on. A young coloured man sat at a table across from her, listening to his iPod as he drank a cappuccino. An elderly woman coughed and sneezed as she had a donut and latte. A young woman cuddling a sleeping baby chatted in Spanish on her cell phone.

What am I doing here? I should be at work, Alison thought, as terror swept through her and grief for the privileged life she'd lost caught her in a vice-like grip. She was jobless, in a recession that was verging on a depression, and she was only one of thousands. She needed to get her act together and sort something out fast.

She finished her coffee, paid her bill and hurried out, feeling flutters of nervy panic envelop her. She walked along in the flurries of snow, head bent, to the grocery store, where she bought some basic supplies to stock up her fridge. She'd want to start cooking for herself a lot more; eating out was a luxury she'd be cutting back on. Her heart sank at the thought. Cooking was not Alison's forte and didn't interest her in the slightest. She'd cooked an omelette the day before and managed to burn her pan. The omelette, which was tasteless and rubbery from overcooking, had ended up in the bin. She handed over her precious dollars to the woman at the till. 'Sure is cold out theah today, honey, could ya close the doah on ya way out? Ma poor bones do ache in this weather. Ma son asked me to come and mind the store 'cause his manager's wife's havin' a baby, and the girl that helps is out sick. I'm gonna tell him he needs to put more heatin' in this place.' The chatty black woman smiled at her.

'You do that.' Alison smiled back, taking her brown-bagged provisions off the counter and making way for an elderly Italian man, who lifted his cap to her and inclined his head politely.

What a gentleman, she thought as she closed the door behind her. She'd only ever seen that in films. It was such a nice, mannerly thing to do. The small gesture lifted her heart and she made her way across the street with her shopping. Good manners were such a hallmark of her parents' generation, thought Alison, suddenly missing her mam and dad, and home. She'd unpack her shopping and phone them, she decided as she hastened up the steps of her new building and took out her keys. The door opened before she had inserted the key in the lock.

'Oh!' she said, startled, as she almost bumped into a tall, bejeaned man in a chunky dark-green sweater and a baseball cap who was barrelling out the door.

'Oops! Sorry about that,' he apologized, taking a step back.

'No problem.' She couldn't help smiling. He had such a good-humoured, craggy face – with gorgeous blue eyes, she noted.

'You're Irish,' he declared.

'Right back at ya!' She laughed at his rich west-of-Ireland brogue. 'Connemara?'

'Drat! I thought I'd got rid of the accent,' he joked, holding out his hand. 'John Joseph Connelly, or JJ to my friends.'

'Alison Dunwoody,' she reciprocated, giving him an equally firm handclasp.

'Well, Alison Dunwoody, I'm delighted to meet you, and these gangsters here are Frankie and Fintan McManus.' He indicated in the direction of a van she'd just noticed parked on the street. 'They're giving me a hand to move in.' Two men in their thirties raised their hands in salute.

'Howya, Alison?' greeted the one called Fintan. The other one just nodded shyly.

'Oh, you're moving in. I've just moved in and spent my first night here. I was over buying provisions across the street.' She clutched one of the brown bags, which was beginning to slip, more tightly.

'I'm up on the third floor, so there'll be a bit of toing and froing for a while. I hope you won't mind.'

''Course not. Glad I'm not up there – one flight of stairs was enough for me.' Alison laughed.

'So you're on the first floor, if I need to borrow some sugar for my coffee.' Her neighbour's eyes crinkled up in a smile.

'Don't use it,' she smiled back. 'It's bad for you.'

'Oh, don't say that, my dear good woman, you sound like my mother. Everyone needs something that's bad for them.' He winked at her and she laughed.

'Well, coffee's bad for you and I use that, so don't be stuck. I'm 1A,' she added.

'Likewise about being stuck. I'm 3B.'

'Good luck with your moving, see you around,' said Alison, edging past him and climbing the stairs to her first-floor studio.

'Right, lads,' she heard JJ say. 'Let's get a move on and give it a lash,' using a phrase she hadn't heard since she'd left home. It was strangely comforting, listening to his accent and knowing that she now knew at least one person in her building. That was another good thing that had happened today. Esther had always taught her and Olivia that if they were finding the going tough to count at least three good and positive things that had happened in their day.

The polite elderly gentleman had raised his cap to her and made her feel good, she had met JJ Connelly, with his twinkling blue eyes, and she was going to ring home from the call box on the corner, because it would be cheaper and she'd be able to spend longer talking to her parents without feeling she was spending a fortune using her cell phone. All in all, it wasn't the day she had dreaded at all, Alison reflected as she let herself into her new abode and heard the clatter of furniture being lugged up the stairs and the distinctive deep voice of her new neighbour directing operations, with plenty of muffled oaths from Frankie and Fintan.

Chapter 5

'Gran, this is yummy.' Seven-year-old Kate chomped with great appreciation on a tender piece of steak as gravy dribbled down her chin.

'Thank you, darling. Wipe your chin, pet, you've got gravy running down it.' Esther handed her grand-daughter a paper napkin.

'Grandad, will you make a lake for me?' Five-year-old Ellie nudged her grandfather in the ribs.

'Of course I will. Give me your plate.' Liam smiled down at his youngest granddaughter and felt a wave of contentment. He loved when Olivia and her young family spent an afternoon with them. It was like the house breathed life again as childish voices filled the air and laughter and chat and their happy singing and innocent joyfulness infused the bricks and mortar. He made a hollow in Ellie's creamy mash and built up the sides so that it looked like the crater of a volcano, before pouring in some more dark, rich, aromatic gravy. 'Now tuck into that, and it will make you big and strong,' he urged.

'And don't mess,' warned her mother, as Ellie splashed her spoon into it.

'Hurry up, everyone, so we can start the puddings.' Kate was shovelling her dinner into her mouth. Lia, her twin, ate slowly, lost in a daydream, eyes staring into the far distance.

'Slow down, we've plenty of time. We don't want you getting indigestion,' Esther advised, amused. Typical Kate, no patience for anything. She reminded her of Alison sometimes. Lia was more like Olivia, restrained, logical, working everything out for herself.

'Thanks for doing dinner, Mam. I managed to make inroads on the small bedroom before . . . er . . .' Olivia caught herself just in time – she'd been about to say 'before Alison comes', '. . . before Christmas,' she amended. The sooner her mother's surprise party was over, the better. She was petrified that she was going to let something slip.

'Are we having apple crumble for dessert?' Lia finished her dinner and placed her knife and fork neatly together on her plate.

'What do you think?' Esther slipped her arm around the little girl and gave her a cuddle. Lia nestled into her grandmother's shoulder and said matter-of-factly, 'I love you, Gran.'

'Me too,' echoed Kate. 'And you too, Grandad,' she added thoughtfully.

'An' me an' me.' Ellie was not to be outdone.

Olivia felt a calm come over her. Certainly today had been a bit fraught, but moments like this more than made up for it, and she was keenly grateful for them, aware that these were precious times for grandparents and grandchildren. She had once heard a child psychologist say that a loving relationship with grandparents had the most profound effect on children and added to their sense of wellbeing and security. She could see it with her own daughters. They were supremely confident of their grandparents' love and Lia's unprompted declaration came straight from the heart. She could see the delight in her mother's eyes, and that alone made all the hassle of the day worth it.

'And we love you. You're the best girls, aren't they, Liam?' Esther reached out and squeezed her husband's hand.

'The best. So good, in fact, I think a trip to Nolan's is in order after the puddings are made.' The children's eyes lit up in childish glee. Nolan's was the village newsagent's, and a visit with their grandad *always* meant treats.

'Yesss!' said Ellie, punching the air enthusiastically. The adults hid their grins.

'Your grandparents have you spoilt rotten.' Olivia began to gather the plates. 'Say thank you for your dinner.'

'Thank you, Gran,' they chorused obediently.

'That dinner went down fast,' Esther remarked.

'Yes – hurry, Gran, we want to make the puddings. We hope you won't be having coffee after the dessert.' Lia got straight to the point. Esther laughed at their eagerness. 'Puddings first then coffee,' she promised.

Ten minutes later, the dessert was eaten, with many approving comments and scraping of dishes and licking of spoons, and there was a race to clear the table for the big event. Aprons were put on with eager anticipation, the robing ceremony as serious as any in an operating theatre, as strings were tied around the front of waists and, in Ellie's case, double-wrapped right around her. She was such a little elf of a child, Esther thought, kissing the top of her curly head as she stood on the half-stool beside her ready for action.

'I'll leave you women to the work. Call me when it's time to make a wish.' Liam tucked his paper under his arm and headed for the sitting room.

'Yes, this is ladies' work,' Lia assured him, much to his amusement.

'Yes, men are good for putting out the bins and screwing things. My dad is very good at screwing. I bet you are too,' Ellie declared airily, twirling her wooden spoon around like a baton.

Olivia gave a snort and quickly turned away, wishing Michael was with them to see his reaction to this high praise.

'I hope so.' Liam caught Esther's eye, and she struggled to keep her face straight.

'Right, off with you and leave us to our ladies' work,' she instructed her husband. 'Now girls, give each other some room there, spread out at either side of the table, and we'll start on the fruit,' she said, like a general instructing his troops. 'First we have to cut the cherries – be careful with the knives.' Olivia, like the good second-in-command that she was, divided out the cherries equally between the trio, and the work began in earnest, cutting and halving, and arranging artistically on their chopping boards.

The big platter of raisins and sultanas was placed in the centre of the table and the chopped green and red glacé cherries and mixed peel added, bringing glorious colour to the sticky mixture.

Everyone got a chance to whisk an egg, and sieve some flour, and as Esther showed the children what to do, she caught Olivia's eye, and mother and daughter smiled at each other, very much aware that they were creating wonderful heartwarming memories for the three little girls, just as mothers and grandmothers before them had done for them.

The wind howled down the chimney, keening like a banshee, and deluges of rain battered the windows, but the kitchen was warm and snug with the smell of whiskey and fruit wafting around the table. Esther felt a pang of loneliness as she thought of Alison. Had her daughter any notion of what a rare afternoon this was for their family, or would she have been at all interested in assisting, had she been here? She sighed and offered up a little prayer for her younger daughter and gave an added one of thanks for all her own good fortune.

Eventually, the mixture was ready to be spooned into the creamy, speckled pudding bowls which Esther had used for many, many years. 'Time for the wishing ceremony,' Kate declared solemnly. 'Get Grandad quick.'

Ellie was down off her stool in a flash and she hurried to get Liam. 'Grandad! Grandad! Come on, come on,' she yelled, dancing with excitement. 'You can wish for anything you want, but you're not to tell what it is.'

Liam swept her up in his arms and came back into the kitchen, sniffing appreciatively. 'Ummm! Let me inspect to see if it's up to standard,' he said, winking at Esther. He poked and stirred and ate a cherry as his granddaughters watched him anxiously, awaiting his verdict.

'Perfect,' he declared. 'The best ever. Time to give it a stir and make a wish. Who's first?'

'Youngest first,' Olivia decreed as they all clamoured for the wooden spoon. It was a most solemn occasion. Each of them took their turn, their little faces earnest as they stirred and wished for their heart's desire. Esther was about to take her turn when the phone rang.

'Hi, Mam, how are things? What's happening?' Alison's voice floated down the line clear as a bell.

'Ah, darlin', what perfect timing. We've just finished mixing the puddings, and we're all here making our wishes,' Esther exclaimed. 'What a pity you can't be with us, Alison.' Her heart ached with loneliness. She had such a longing to see her younger daughter, it was almost physical.

'Is Olivia with you? Are the girls there?'

'Yes, we're all here. Your father has just given the mix his seal of approval and the wishing ceremony is taking place.' Esther smiled down at her granddaughters, who were waiting impatiently for her to make her wish, so they could spoon the mixture into the bowls.

'I'll make a wish for you, Auntie Alison,' Kate offered loudly.

'Did you hear that, Alison?'

'I did. I'd love you to make a wish for me, Kate,' Alison said as Esther held the phone out for them all to hear the exchange. 'Give it a good stir for me,' she urged.

'Me too, me too,' clamoured Ellie, grabbing the spoon.

'Mommm!!' Kate protested. 'I said I was doing it.'

'You can all do one,' Olivia said, as it looked as though a row was going to break out.

'Wow! Three wishes – how lucky am I?' Alison's voice drifted over the pudding basin as her nieces each gave a vigorous stir, trying to outdo each other with their vim.

'There, it's done,' Esther assured Alison when it was finished. 'You don't usually ring in the afternoon. You're not off work sick or anything are you? Are you ringing from a call box?' she queried. 'I can hear traffic.' It was strange that her daughter should ring during the day. It was usually night time in Ireland when she phoned, generally being too busy in the morning to make personal phone calls.

'Emm . . . yeah, I was just heading uptown to a meeting and had a few minutes to spare, and I have to go to a function tonight so I just thought I'd give you a quick call. The signal's not great on my phone here so I used a booth. I wanted to see how you were doing after the flu.'

'Much better, love, much better,' Esther said warmly, touched by her daughter's concern. 'How are you? Up to your eyes as usual? Gadding about having the high life with Jonathan? Are you off anywhere exotic this year?'

'Er . . . just staying in New York,' Alison fibbed, hating having to lie but not wanting to worry her parents about how utterly her circumstances had changed. Jonathan might not even be on the scene by Christmas if her altered situation impacted too much on their relationship.

'Do you want to say hello to your father?' Esther asked. 'He's here helping out.'

'I'd love to. Thanks, Mam. Enjoy making the puddings. I'll talk to you soon.' Alison was relieved she didn't have to tell any more vague untruths to her mother.

'Hello, Alison, how are you doing?' Liam took the phone. 'How are things in the Big Apple? Are the banking dramas having any effect on you? It's dreadful here, Anglo's gone belly up.'

'Umm . . . I know – I lost my shares there, the greedy scumbags.' Alison was thrown off guard. She longed to drop the façade and confide that *she'd* gone belly up and lost her job as well as her investments. She was trying to keep the feelings of stomach-lurching apprehension at bay as her savings diminished with heart-stopping rapidity and the affluent lifestyle she had known became a mere dream. Her success story was over, her family would be so disappointed – *for* her, not *in* her – if she told them the truth. It would be so easy to blurt it out, but what good would it do? It would only upset them, and she didn't want to do that. She'd keep quiet for another while, maybe things would take a turn for the better.

'Yeah, it's all a bit mad here too, Dad, we're just hoping things might begin to stabilize now that Obama's plan has been passed by Congress,' she managed.

'Tough times, love. You know, you should think about buying a place at home, just so you'd have a roof over your head if you ever wanted to come back. Property prices are way down. Now's the time to buy. Or if you're planning on staying stateside, buy there. That's a very hefty rent you pay out in New York. It's dead money,' Liam advised.

'Yeah, good thinking, Dad. The next time I'm home I'll see what the scene is like.' She tried to keep her tone airy. 'Is Olivia still there? I'll say a quick hello before I head off.'

'Yes, love, here she is. Mind yourself now and keep in touch. I'll email you tonight.'

'OK, Dad, bye.' Liam handed the phone to Olivia.

'Hi, Alison, pudding mix is looking good,' Olivia said.

'Sounds like fun,' her sister said wistfully.

'It is, but the washing-up awaits!'

'Is everything on track for the party?'

'Yeah, no prob,' Olivia said non-committally.

'Right, see you next week so.'

'Is it snowing?' Olivia changed the subject hastily, aware of their mother's keen hearing.

'Pelting down. I better go – I'll call you over the weekend. Let me hear another wish being made.'

Olivia held the phone over the table. 'Right, every-one, hands on the wooden spoon and everyone make a last wish for Alison,' she ordered.

Eager hands grasped the spoon and stirred it in a circle in the big basin of pudding mix. 'For Auntie Alison,' her nieces yelled as Liam placed his hand over his wife's and gave it a little squeeze, knowing instinc-tively that Esther was wishing Alison was there with them. She felt a stab of loneliness as she took the phone to say goodbye to Alison and hung up.

'Perfect,' Liam said briskly as they gave a last decisive stir before handing his wife back the wooden spoon. She watched her three granddaughters spooning pudding mixture into the bowls. Liam was helping Ellie, grey head bent close to blond curly one. Ellie's tongue was sticking out of the corner of her mouth as she concentrated intently on the job in hand. Lia spooned slowly, carefully, not wanting to drop any of the mixture, while Kate lashed it in any which way, in her usual carefree gung ho manner. They all had such different personalities, Esther thought fondly as she watched each bowl fill up. Olivia was gathering up the dishes to bring them over to the sink. Esther began filling the dishwasher. She was a lucky woman, to be surrounded by her family. Her daughters were reared and doing well for themselves, her granddaughters were the joy of her life, and her husband was her greatest blessing. How many women hitting seventy had what she had? she thought gratefully, trying to banish the frisson of sadness Alison's phone call had brought. Her daughter had sounded tired, as if she was making an effort to be bright and breezy for them; maybe it was because she'd lost her bank investments. That had to be disheartening. All that hard work for nothing because a small circle of greedy people who felt the rules didn't apply to them had behaved with an arrogance and avariciousness that was beyond belief. Alison had worked damn hard to get where she was. Perhaps that was the problem, maybe she was working way *too* hard and it was getting on top of her. But definitely today she hadn't been her bright, bubbly self, and Esther couldn't help but worry.

Chapter 6

Alison hung the phone back in its cradle after managing a subdued 'Thanks,' and rooted in her bag for a tissue. She felt incredibly lonely. She could just imagine the fun, laughter and excitement in the big warm kitchen at home. They were five hours ahead of her, and her day stretched out in a long, dull vista that made her feel strangely lonely, unsure and apprehensive. Her earlier positivity had disappeared after speaking to her family. She'd had her post redirected to her new building, and there had been no comfort in her mail delivery this morning: utility bills and job refusals and some junk mail. She was going to have to try and get a job waitressing if something didn't come up soon, she thought glumly.

'Now stop!' she said sternly to herself as she headed back to her new pad. She wasn't going to wait for her friends to come to help her unpack; she was going to make a start on her unpacking right this minute. They'd been good enough to help her move her stuff. She needed to just get on with things. It was imperative to keep busy, then she wouldn't have to think about the disaster her life had suddenly become. Right now she would give anything to be at home with her family, making Christmas puddings. In fact, right now she wished she were a child again, with nothing to worry about, cocooned in the love and safety of home.

She could see the Irish guys were back with another load of boxes and belongings for JJ's place. Impulsively, she headed into the deli and ordered four coffees to go and a bag of cookies. It was surely time for them to have a coffee break. It would be a neighbourly thing to do. The kind of thing you'd do at home, she thought, perking up at the thought of having someone to talk to and have a laugh with. She carried the cardboard coffee-holder carefully as she jaywalked across the street. Frankie, the short, wiry one, was leaning against the van having a smoke. 'Are you on for a coffee? I thought you could do with a break,' she said cheerily.

'Hey, that's decent of you. I'll give the lads a shout – or do you want to come up to JJ's?'

'Are you inviting strange women up to my crib, bro?' a deep voice behind them said.

'Your new neighbour here bought us coffee, so yeah, bro,' Frankie joshed back.

'Well, thank you, Ms Dunwoody. Let me take that. We don't want you spilling it. Will you make it up the three flights?' JJ slagged.

'I go to the gym, I'll make it,' she said confidently.

'You're a fit-lookin' woman all right,' Frankie asserted. 'And that's more than I can say for myself.'

'After you,' JJ said politely when they reached 3B.

'Oh, it's big! Much bigger than mine,' exclaimed Alison, walking down a hallway that led into a large airy room with two long sash windows to the front and a smaller window to the side.

'This is a one-bed. There are two one-bed apartments on this floor and the floor underneath. Your floor and the ground floor are the studios,' JJ explained. 'A friend of mine owns this building. I helped him renovate it. I'm in the process of buying a fairly

71

rundown clapboard house in Westchester that I'm going to renovate in my spare time. I'm going to live in a trailer there once the deal goes through and spring comes.'

'Oh! You're in the building trade?' queried Alison, gazing around at some beautiful pieces of furniture which, to her eye, looked very expensive.

'I'm a carpenter by trade, but I specialize in bespoke furniture,' JJ said as he handed her a coffee, and offered one each to Frankie and Fintan.

'Wow, that's an amazing table.' Alison ran her finger along a circular rosewood table that gleamed even in the leaden daylight that filtered through the voile curtains. There were six chairs, too, carved ornately and padded in a rich burgundy material. JJ Connelly had impressive taste, she reflected, noting the elegant bookshelves awaiting their treasures and the slim, matching rosewood, glass-fronted cabinets that stood at each corner of the wall, the round table between them.

'Glad you like it,' he said crisply, blue eyes glinting at her. He'd taken off his peaked sports cap, and his thick, dark-chestnut hair was boyishly tousled.

'Have a cookie?' she offered, remembering she'd bought them.

'Don't mind if I do.' He took one out of the bag she proffered and wolfed it down with a slug of coffee. Alison offered the bag to the two F's, as she'd privately christened them, and they gave them short shrift.

'So what line of business are you in, Alison?' JJ eyed her speculatively.

'I was in the financial sector.' She shrugged.

'Was?' He arched an eyebrow at her.

'Yep. I lost my job a few weeks ago. The firm I was working for collapsed after the Madoff scandal. Went to work one morning and we were all told to go home, the company was bankrupt. So that was that. Jobless, with not much prospect of getting another one at the moment. I've sublet my apartment uptown and taken this one while my friend, who lives here, is in LA. I took it for three months. If I don't get a job by then, I guess I'll have to quit America and go home, or see what comes up else-where,' she explained.

'That's tough,' he said quietly as the two F's murmured agreement.

'Yeah, it's kind of ironic – my speciality is wealth management,' she added lightly.

'Ah well, ye wouldn't be dealing with the likes of us, Alison,' Frankie grinned. 'We don't have any wealth worth talking about, do we, lads?'

'Yer right there,' Fintan agreed.

'My sister was made redundant recently, in London.' JJ frowned. 'Worked for twenty years with the same company, gave her heart and soul to them, and wham! Out the door without even a word of thanks. You're only a commodity in business. I used to tell her so when she took work home with her. "You'll get no thanks for it," I told her, and I was right – and I take no pleasure being proved right either. I bet you were the same.'

'Yeah, a bit, I put in the extra hours, but I felt it *was* appreciated,' retorted Alison defensively.

'Listen, my dear good woman, and take this to heart for the next job you go to, it's every man for himself in business, and profit is the bottom line. It's a rare thing to find humanity in the cut and thrust of the corporate world. I have to say, from what I've seen in business, I'm very glad I work for myself.' JJ eyed her quizzically. 'Did you have a nice pad uptown?'

'Two bedrooms, separate kitchen and a little balcony. I loved it. I was gutted leaving it,' she admitted. 'I'm really hoping to get another position asap and get back to it.'

'The recession won't last for ever. They're talking recovery already. I swear to God that's what I love about the States. It's all so positive, even when things are at their worst. At home it's all gloom and doom. The media are so negative over there, it always shocks me when I go back.'

'You'd nearly shoot yourself if you lived at home, listening to that pessimism day in day out,' Fintan interjected as he took another cookie and scoffed it in one mouthful, crumbs scattering all over his fleece and his bushy red beard.

'I'm going home next week for my mother's seventieth. Couldn't be worse timing. I won't be saying anything about losing my job though. My dad's been on at me to buy property for years, he says rent is dead money, and he's right, I suppose. It's too late now though,' Alison confided. It was so odd: she felt very comfortable with the three Irishmen, and having a conversation with them was almost a treat. She hadn't realized just how lonely it was being unemployed, having nowhere to go and no one to interact with during the day.

'Well, look at it like this – if you'd bought at the peak of the boom, you'd be in negative equity,' JJ said kindly, 'although I have to say, in general, I'm a fan of bricks and mortar myself. Don't trust the stock market.'

'Right now neither do I. I've taken such a hit with my investments and bonuses.' Alison nodded in agreement, draining her coffee. 'I guess I better let you get on and finish unpacking. I've to make a start myself. I've boxes everywhere.'

'Thanks for the coffee, neighbour,' JJ grinned, showing even, white teeth.

'Thanks, Alison, nice to meet ya,' and 'Good on ya,' the two F's added.

'You're welcome,' Alison assured them, deciding that she was going to make her studio as nice as possible, just in case JJ Connelly ever came to her door looking to borrow sugar. She'd buy some just in case.

Once she made a start, it wasn't so bad, and there was a degree of satisfaction in emptying each box, putting away her belongings and beginning to feel an ownership of her new abode. Once the empty cardboard boxes were flattened, the place didn't look so cluttered, and she was quite pleased at the homely ambiance she created by putting her books on the bookshelves and her lamps at each window. Alison loved soft lighting in her home space. It relaxed her and made the place feel cosy, especially in the viciously cold winters of the past few years. Most of the offices she had worked in had fluorescent lighting, which she hated.

She stared around after she'd emptied the last box into her by now bulging closet and wondered could she follow up on Melora's suggestion to place a swathe of cream curtain material, to drop in soft folds from the archway that divided the bedroom area from the small sitting room. She could ask JJ. He was a carpenter. It wouldn't take long to stick a curtain rail across the top of the arch.

Melora, minimalist to the last, had put most of her possessions, including her designer clothes, bags and shoes, in storage, all carefully wrapped and labelled. She intended coming back to New York when the winter was over with either a prospective husband or, failing that, a new job in wealth management. No recession was going to get the better of her; she'd emailed Alison telling her she already had a date, having only arrived in LA a week previously.

'You go, girl,' Alison had emailed back in admiration.

Melora was very anxious to get married, as were most of Alison's single friends in New York. It was all about the date and the man, or meeting that special someone, or wondering was the man you were dating really into you. Sometimes Alison wondered if she had a gene missing. Or, she pondered guiltily, was she a bit shallow? She liked dating, but it wasn't the end of the world if there wasn't a man in her life. She hadn't had much time to get into a serious relationship in her twenties, between work and college. But over the last few years she'd had two relationships that had ended because the guys felt she was more committed to her job than she was to them. What was so wrong with loving your work? If it was the other way around and she'd felt they were more committed to their jobs than they were to her, it would have been a perfectly acceptable scenario for them and she would have been labelled 'needy'.

Jonathan suited her perfectly. They had fun, the sex was OK, she wasn't in danger of losing her heart to him – and that was good also, she felt. Losing your heart left you out of control and it was bad enough being out of a job and having temporarily lost control of her career, without losing control of her emotions. That would be a total disaster.

She heard clattering down the stairs and stuck her head out the door. It was Fintan, the red-haired, bearded one of the trio.

'Are ya OK there, Alison?' he said in his broad, rich brogue.

'I thought it might be JJ. I was just going to ask might he be able to stick a curtain rail up for me? Do you think he'd mind?' she ventured, uncharacteristically hesitant.

'Yerra not at all, girl. Show me where you want it and I'll sthick it up for you.' His accent reminded her so much of home she felt a pang of homesickness.

'It was just here over the arch, to close up the bedroom bit,' she explained, leading him into the studio. He studied the archway and reached up and gave it a tap.

'Hmmm, thought it might be plasterboard, but it's fairly solid,' he said knowledgeably. 'You get the pole you want and I'll do that for ye no problem.'

'Thanks a million and please charge me the going rate,' she said hastily.

'Arrah that won't take ten seconds, woman, would ye whist about the going rate.' He laughed, showing a flash of white teeth through his beard.

'Well, I don't want to take advantage. You don't know me,' she demurred.

'If I wasn't happily married, you could take advantage of me any time,' he slagged as he made his way down her narrow hall. 'Here's my card. Let me know when ye have the pole and I'll sort it for ye.' He handed her a cream business card. 'See ye.' And then he was gone, pounding down the stairs until the front door closed and there was silence.

'Fintan McManus, Builder's Providers', she read, with an address in Queens. And a cell and landline number. She'd get the pole tomorrow, it would give her something to do, she decided, yawning. She was really tired all of a sudden. It was late in the afternoon, the snow was whispering down past her window and the leaden sky was darkening the apartment. She yawned again. Usually she was full of energy, but this lassitude, this weariness, had happened several times in the past few weeks, since the shock of being made unemployed.

One of her friends, Stella, who was a psychotherapist,

had told her it was normal under the circumstances. 'Losing your job is a bereavement of sorts. Your whole psyche is in upheaval. You're traumatized. Your sleep patterns are gone to pot. The mind and body need to adjust and accept this new and unaccustomed situation, so when the tiredness comes, give in to it and rest, it's not laziness, Alison,' Stella had insisted when Alison had assured her she wouldn't be caught dead taking a nap in the afternoon.

Today, though, she was just going to work through her guilt and lie down and flick through a magazine for ten minutes. She'd slept so badly the previous night in the strange bed and unfamiliar environment, it was no wonder she was tired. She kicked off her shoes and curled on top of the bed, pulled a soft Tommy Hilfiger throw over her, and began to flick through *Vanity Fair*, her favourite magazine. The studio was lovely and warm, the lamplight casting soft shadows on the walls and, outside, the snow fell steadily and unrelentingly, blanketing the city. The noise of the traffic was gently muffled, and she fell fast asleep.

A knocking on the door woke her, and she shot up, dazed and disorientated. The clock on her bedside locker showed it was after seven. She'd been asleep for more than three hours. She jumped off the bed, ran her fingers through her hair, hurried out to the door and unlocked the various locks.

'Did I wake you up?' JJ stood there with a cream curtain pole in one hand and a tool kit in the other. 'Oopps! Sorry – maybe you have someone with you? Fintan told me about your curtain-pole conversation, and I was passing a hardware store on the way home and stopped and got this. It will go with the colour we painted all the apartments in, if your friend hasn't redecorated,' he said briskly. 'But listen, I can come back another time.' He turned to go.

'No, no, there's no one here. I fell asleep for a few minutes, didn't sleep so good in a strange bed last night, and Melora didn't change the colours.' She stifled a yawn, stepping back to let him in. She was mortified at having been caught snoozing.

'The same fate probably awaits me tonight,' JJ said. 'Although I do have my own bed with me. But the creaks and rattles in the building and the noise outside will be different to what I'm used to. It's always like that at first when you move.'

'That's *exactly* it. And I had a doorman before as well. It's that extra bit of security that you get used to.

Did you live in an apartment too?' she asked as he followed her in.

'Nope. I had a house in Rockaway, and I've sold it to buy the place I was telling you about.'

'A house! You *will* find it a bit different then,' Alison remarked. 'Are you married? Do you have kids?'

'Was married. No kids,' he said succinctly.

'Oh!' she said. Was married . . . Did that mean he was divorced? she wondered.

'Right, where do you want this? Is it OK for you?' He was all business-like.

'It's fine, fine. Thanks so much for going to so much trouble.' She wished she'd had a chance to brush her hair. She knew she must look a sight. 'I was just going to hang a curtain here,' she said, flustered, as she led him through the alcove, aware of the tossed blanket and pillows and the magazine face down on the bed. How lazy he must think her. It was so unfair. She couldn't think of the last time she'd fallen asleep on the bed on a weekday. And why was she so bothered anyway about what he might think? What was wrong with her?

'This won't take a jiffy. Can I stand on one of your kitchen chairs, or are they delicate little things?' JJ asked.

'I'm not in the posh apartment like you. I don't have kitchen chairs. My kitchen's just a little galley,' she reminded him, throwing her eyes up to heaven as she regained some equilibrium.

'Sorry, forgot you were slumming it,' he teased.

'How about the ottoman at the end of the bed?' she suggested.

'Grand job.' He bent down and untied his shoes. He had lovely thick hair, Alison noted, and he was very broad-shouldered. Even in his stocking feet he was over six feet tall. He was wearing a light-blue shirt tucked into his jeans and had a lean, easy grace about him as he slid the ottoman over to the arch and stood up on it.

'If you just hold these for me, I'd be obliged,' he said, handing her some screws and rawl plugs. He took a slim, fold-up wooden ruler from his hip pocket and made a quick measurement.

Nice ass, Alison thought, as he stretched to the left a little. He made two discreet pencil marks, then got down and picked up his drill. 'Just a little bit of dust – is that OK?'

'No probs.'

Five minutes later, her curtain pole hung neatly across the top of the arch and he was packing away his drill. 'Ummm, how much do I owe you, JJ?' Alison inserted a note of firm authority in her voice. Fintan might have offered to do the job for nothing, but JJ had gone and bought the curtain pole as well.

'Have you eaten yet?' He glanced up at her as he tied his shoelaces.

'Er . . . no,' she replied, wondering what had that to do with the cost of buying and putting up a curtain pole.

'Right, me neither. How about ordering in a Chinese, there's a really good one a few blocks down that we used when we were working on this place. You can pay for dinner,' he suggested casually. 'I have a bottle of Bin 555 upstairs.'

'Well . . . well, sure if that's what you want.' She was completely thrown.

'It would be kinda neighbourly. I don't know any of the other inmates and I wouldn't have to eat on my own here the first night, and it might help you get over your "paying for the job" fixation!' he said easily.

Alison laughed. 'Melora said the people here are nice enough, except for some old bag on the second floor who's a bit nosy.'

'Ah yes, that would be the redoubtable Mrs Wadeski, who has already taken me to task about the noise I was making arranging my furniture. A formidable woman indeed, and with a moustache that would put a bristle brush to shame.' He grinned.

'God, you're awful,' Alison snorted, laughing.

'So how about I put this stuff away, get the number of the Oriental Orchid for you, bring down the wine, and we order dinner. The house-special chow mein is particularly good.'

'OK. I haven't been bossed around this much since I left home,' she retorted, feeling she should make some sort of a stand.

'It's good for ya, Dunwoody. Stick on the kettle while we're waiting, I'd murder a cuppa.'

'OK, Connelly, I'll let you away with it this once,' she warned as he finished tying his laces and stood up.

'Leave the teabag in the mug for me, I don't want wishy-washy tea' was his parting shot as he left with his tool kit.

Alison stood under the arch shaking her head. Her life had taken on a peculiarly surreal quality. This time yesterday she was surrounded by boxes in a building where she knew no one, in a strange part of town and feeling absolutely isolated and alone. And in the space of twelve hours, her little studio was cosy and comfortable, if somewhat bursting at the seams, and she was hungry and going to have a meal with a tall, good-humoured Irishman who bossed her around like nobody's business – and she'd had a long afternoon nap to boot. It was one of the strangest days she'd had since she'd come to New York, but for the first time since she lost her job the terrifying flutters of panic and apprehension she'd been experiencing had faded somewhat.

She ran a brush through her hair, squirted on some 212, slipped into her loafers, straightened the bed and went out to the kitchen to organize plates, glasses and cutlery. The kitchen had a small counter that doubled as a worktop and two stools sat against it. They could eat there or in on the sofa, side by side. She decided to set places at the counter. Side by side on the sofa was too intimate with a relative stranger, although she had to admit JJ was very easy company and she felt relaxed with him for some odd reason. Probably because she was a bit vulnerable at the moment and it was nice to be with someone from home, she decided.

She boiled the kettle, stuck a teabag in the mug and filled it with water.

His sharp rat-a-tat-tat on the door made her smile. JJ wasn't a doorbell man, it seemed. 'Here's the menu, see what you want. I'm having the spring rolls and the house-special chow mein.' Her guest handed her the menu. 'Give me a corkscrew and I'll open the wine to let it breathe while you're making your mind up.'

'How high *exactly* would you like me to jump?' she said tartly, and he laughed.

'Don't mind me, my dear woman. I had three older sisters and I had to stand up for myself. Old habits die hard.'

'Is that right? So you're spoilt rotten then,' Alison observed. 'Do you still want the tea if you're having wine?'

'If it's no trouble,' he said with pretended docility. 'I love the tay, as they say at home.'

'Oh God, I've no sugar,' she suddenly remembered.

'I brought my own,' he said smugly, handing her a bag. 'You might as well keep it here in case I pop in for the odd cuppa!' He put three heaped spoonfuls into the mug.

'Hey! That's way too much.' She was shocked.

'But lovely sweet tay.' He grinned, pouring in some milk and taking a slug. 'There's nothing in the world to beat a decent cup of tea. Hurry on and pick something – the stomach's falling out of me.'

He opened the wine as she perused the menu; she decided on some prawn toast and the shredded duck. 'You order and give your number and then you'll be on their computer,' he advised, sitting on the stool across from her, long legs stretched out in front of him.

'I don't intend staying here for long,' she retorted. 'I want my apartment back and I want a job.'

'What's for you won't pass you by,' he said calmly.

'My mother says that to me and my sister all the time.' Alison smiled at the old saying as she picked up the phone to call in the order.

Two hours, a Chinese takeaway and half a bottle of red wine later, she was sprawled on one end of the sofa, with JJ at the other end, and they were both yawning their heads off.

'God, woman, you're contagious. Stop yawning, for heaven's sake. I'm going to my bed, I've to be up at six.' He hauled himself up off the sofa and stood looking down at her. 'Very nice evening, neighbour.'

'Enjoyed it myself,' she reciprocated, standing up to let him out.

'Good luck on the job-hunting front,' he said as he stood at the door.

'Fingers crossed. Sleep well in your new gaff.'

'I'll do my best.' He smiled. 'Goodnight, Dunwoody.'

'Goodnight, Connelly, and thanks,' she said warmly.

'See ya around,' he said, and then he was loping down the landing and taking the stairs two at a time. Alison closed the door and put on the three locks. She'd really enjoyed her evening, she mused as she carried their dishes to the sink and put the takeaway cartons in the refuse bin. They'd chatted, mostly about home, and the time had gone by so fast she couldn't believe it was almost eleven. She heard the front door opening downstairs, and a door on the ground floor opening a few minutes later. The tenant above her had had a bath and the water was gurgling down the pipes. Last night she'd been tense and agitated when she got into bed. Tonight was different, and it wasn't just the wine, she reflected as she switched off the lights in the kitchen and sitting room, swiftly undressed, pulled on her PJs, slid into bed and heaved the duvet up over her ears. Tonight she was more relaxed because she knew JJ was upstairs, and it was nice to have someone she knew in the building. She'd made a new friend today. Someone she felt very comfortable with. Why had his marriage broken up? she wondered. Had he done the dirty on his wife, or had his wife done the dirty on him? He seemed a very decent bloke, the type of man her mother would like. Alison smiled in the dark. Esther hadn't been too taken with Jonathan when she'd met him for the first time on her last visit.

'He takes a lot of care over his appearance, doesn't he?' she'd remarked when Jonathan had apologized for keeping them late for drinks because his manicurist had been running late.

Somehow or other, Alison couldn't imagine JJ Connelly going to a manicurist, although she'd noted that his nails were cut short and were very clean. No, she decided, there was nothing of the metrosexual about her neighbour upstairs. He was a real, solid, down-to-earth man with a great sense of humour and a tasty ass in his blue jeans. And handy to have around, which was more than could ever be said for her non-exclusive boyfriend, who wouldn't know one end of a hammer from another, she thought in amusement, wondering why he hadn't phoned.

Five minutes later, she was fast asleep, and she slept so well she never even heard the front door downstairs close at six the following morning, as a tall, lean, blue-eyed man glanced up at her window with a hint of a smile before getting into his jeep and heading off to work.

Chapter 7

'It's an eggbox!' Jonathan Bailey gazed around studio 1A, a mixture of dismay and disdain darkening his fine-boned, thin, angular face.

'It's not that bad,' Alison exclaimed defensively.

'I've been in bigger hotel rooms!' he scoffed, peering into the tiny kitchen. 'God, look at the size of your fridge, you wouldn't fit half a dozen bottles of champers in there.'

'Oh, give it a rest, Jon,' Alison said wearily. 'I know it's small, but it's all I can afford – I'm jobless, remember. No nice fat salary coming in.'

It was the day before she was due to fly home, and her boyfriend had arrived back from LA looking tanned and rested. He was going to bring her to dinner in Tsar Ivan's, one of her favourite Russian restaurants, and then they were going clubbing in Recession, a new hip club on the Upper East Side. He had a Town Car waiting outside. He was dressed in a grey Armani suit with a ruby-red shirt open at the neck. A real LA playboy outfit, she reflected as she slipped on a black cashmere coat that had cost an arm and a leg and picked up a cream-silk hand-painted scarf to wrap around her neck. She was wearing cream Jimmy Choos and carried a cream diamanté-studded clutch. Her hair was piled up on her head, with loose tendrils falling around her face, and her make-up was impeccably applied, the dark, smoky eyeliner empha-sizing her wide green eyes. A familiar rat-a-tat-tat at the door made her jump.

'Hey, Dunwoody, open up,' a deep voice called.

Jonathan looked around, startled. 'Who the hell is that?'

'My upstairs neighbour,' Alison murmured, amused at the look of shock on his face.

'Bit loud, isn't he?' he remarked, as Alison moved past him to open the door.

'Fry-up in 3B, including Clonakilty pudding and Superquinn sausages. Are you interested?' JJ asked, thumbs hooked in his jean pockets. His eyes slid slowly down over her as he took in her appearance. 'Going out?' he enquired, glancing over her shoulder to where Jonathan was standing, frowning.

'Ah yeah. JJ, this is my boyfriend, Jonathan Bailey. Jonathan, this is one of my neighbours, JJ Connelly.'

'Hello, pleased to meet you,' Jonathan said with polite disinterest.

'Likewise,' JJ said, gripping the other man's outstretched hand in a firm handshake. 'One of the lads I work with came back from Ireland this morning with enough rashers, sausages and puddings to feed the state. Frankie and Fintan are upstairs, and we thought you might fancy a bite to eat with us,' he explained.

'We're going out to dinner,' Jonathan drawled.

'So I see. Just a thought, Alison. Enjoy your evening.'

'It's a pity, I wouldn't have minded a few Superquinn sausages,' she said regretfully. 'I haven't had them in yonks. I'm always afraid to bring stuff like that back in case I get caught.'

'Ways and means,' JJ said lightly.

'Well, thanks for thinking of me, and enjoy it and tell the lads to enjoy it too,' she said, thinking she wouldn't have minded going upstairs for a fry-up with the gang.

'Any time. Enjoy your evening. Good to meet you.' He eyeballed Jonathan, who looked taken aback at the flinty stare.

'We should go. The car's outside, and our reservations are for seven thirty. The maître d's got us a table as a favour, this place is booked up weeks in advance,' Jonathan said loftily.

'Don't let me delay you,' JJ said and sprinted up the stairs with panther-like ease.

'How did you meet him and get so friendly?' Jonathan said grumpily as she locked the door behind them and they began to walk down the stairs.

'He moved in the day after I did. I met him and two other Irish chaps on the stairs moving his furniture up. It was nice to talk to someone from home.'

'He calls you by your surname. He called you Dunwoody – isn't that rude?' he sniffed.

'Oh no, not at home, not in the west of Ireland. It's a form of—' She had been going to say 'endearment', but stopped herself. 'It's an Irish thing,' she explained.

'Who are they? Builders?' he said contemptuously.

'They're three really nice guys, Jonathan,' she said sharply, in no humour for his snobbery.

'If you say so,' he retorted, opening the door for her.

'I do,' Alison snapped.

'Any luck on the job scene?' he asked after a while, as they drove around Times Square and headed uptown.

'I had an interview this morning in a stockbroker's in Wall Street – along with a few hundred others, I'm sure.' Alison sighed.

'We let go twenty-five personnel in the West Coast division. It was a rough couple of weeks,' he moaned.

For them, not for you, she thought sarcastically. Every time he'd phoned her, he'd been socializing. 'Poor you,' she said dryly, but he didn't even notice.

'I got you a present, babe,' he said, handing her a small bag.

'Thanks, Jonathan,' she said warmly, suddenly ashamed of her nasty thoughts. It was a small bottle of Nina Ricci eau de toilette. He'd got it in the airport, a rushed buy, a last-minute better-get-her-something sort of a gift, she surmised, and not even the perfume at that. Jonathan was very careful with his money, unless he was splashing out on himself. 'My ex bleeds me dry' was his favourite line.

The driver pulled up outside the Russian restaurant and opened the door for her. It was a bitingly cold night and she shivered as the chill wind wrapped itself around her. The restaurant was warm and dimly lit, all red damask and gilt. It was only half full. What a spoofer Jonathan was, trying to impress JJ with his talk of the maître d' holding the table for him as a special favour.

They ordered Nostoykas – fruit-flavoured vodkas – and read the menu in silence. She chose blinis and stuffed cabbage rolls; he ordered Siberian pelsemi and the Tzyplenok.

'You look great,' he said slowly as the waiter moved away.

'Thanks,' she responded coolly.

'I'm looking forward to our reunion,' he said huskily, reaching out to caress her hand. He leaned across the table and kissed her.

'Later,' she chided. She thought it was crass to kiss in restaurants. It was strange, but the idea of having sex with him later on was a somewhat uninviting prospect, despite the fact they hadn't seen each other for almost three weeks. She doubted very much he'd stayed celibate in LA. And the awful thing was, she suddenly realized she didn't really care. Jonathan had been no help to her at all in her hour of need. He hadn't offered her a room in his four-bed duplex, he hadn't offered to help her find a place to live, and the best he could do was to buy her a tacky little bottle of eau de toilette at LAX.

But that was Jonathan! She knew what he was like. Why should it make a difference to her now? she mused gloomily as the waiter laid their first course in front of them. It must be because she had lost her job and was feeling out of control and vulnerable. Suddenly she wished she was snug in her little studio, listening to the wind whistling outside or, even better, upstairs in 3B with JJ, Frankie and Fintan, having banter and craic and tucking into a fry-up.

'. . . So Yvette said to me that she thinks Gloria is seeing this Goulandris guy, and he's loaded. She's such a bitch, looking for more alimony . . .' Jonathan was on his favourite subject, his ex-wife.

'That's terrible.' She'd heard it all before.

'Oh to hell with them,' he said suddenly. 'Let's go to Colorado for Christmas. We'll have big log fires and spend all day in bed.'

Alison laughed. His impulsiveness was one of the things she'd always enjoyed about him. 'It sounds great, but I can't afford it,' she reminded him.

'Oh yeah, forgot you're strapped for cash. Couldn't you sell a bond or something?' he suggested glumly.

Couldn't you offer to pay for my flight as my Christmas present even? she thought, wondering how she had overlooked his meanness for so long. 'I was thinking I might spend Christmas at home this year, seeing as I don't have a job at the moment,' she said pointedly.

'Oh! You're going to leave me on my own.' His brown, cocker-spaniel eyes had their 'poor me' expression.

'I don't think you'll be on your own exactly, Jonathan. Since when have you *ever* been on your own?' she said acerbically.

'Well, I know, but we have fun, Red.' Red was his nickname for her; he thought it highly original.

'Well, Jonathan, it's like this, I have to tighten my purse strings unfortunately, so I won't be able to have as much fun as I used to, but you go right ahead,' she said crisply.

'That's a nuisance,' he sighed, forking a dumpling into his mouth. She could see him pondering who else could he ask to go to Colorado with him. She really didn't care any more.

'Jonathan, would you mind if I went home? I have the most terrible headache,' Alison fibbed.

'Really? You don't usually get headaches.' He was surprised.

'Flo came to town,' she murmured.

'Oh . . . Oh right. Maybe it would be good to go and lie down then. I'll phone you tomorrow before you go to the airport,' he said hastily.

'Great and . . . thanks for the present.'

'Love ya, babe. Let me get the maître d' to call a cab.' He stood up and escorted her to the foyer.

Five minutes later, she was sitting in a taxi heading across town. Jonathan couldn't get rid of her quick enough, she thought in amusement. Knowing he wasn't going to have a hot and steamy reunion had put the kybosh on the evening for him. She'd lied. Her period hadn't come; she'd just known that she and Jonathan were over. He hadn't even offered to bring her to the airport.

Being non-exclusive had lost its charm; she needed to be a bit more discerning in who she dated from now on. Paying your own way was all very well, but if your so-called 'non-exclusive' boyfriend, whom you'd been dating and sleeping with for almost six months, couldn't even pay your cab fare home, it didn't say much about him . . . or her for putting up with it, she acknowledged. It was all very well being Miss Independence, but she needed to value herself more and value the person she dated, she thought with a dart of shame.

She'd used Jonathan just as much as he'd used her, and it wasn't very nice behaviour really. She thought of Fintan offering to put up her curtain pole, and JJ going out of his way to buy it. She thought of Jonathan's dismissive 'builders' barb. The three Irishmen had a core of decency in them that he would never have. He might have money and a high-flying job in his father's company and an entrée into all the top-end restaurants and clubs coast to coast, but he had no real integrity or moral fibre, as her mother would say.

The next time she dated it would be with a far different type of man, Alison decided, as she paid her cab fare and let herself into her building, glad to shut out the bitter-cold night. She hurried up the stairs and was about to walk down her landing when an impulse took her. It was only gone eight thirty, she noted, glancing at her watch. Taking a deep breath, she took the next flight of stairs, and then the next. The sound of laughter and deep male voices wafted across the landing at the top of the building. And the smell of bacon made her mouth water.

She gave a sharp rat-a-tat-tat on the door. She heard silence descend inside. JJ opened the door in an unusually tentative manner. His face lit up when he saw her.

'Hey, Dunwoody. I thought you were Mrs W. come to tell us we were making too much noise. What are you doing here?'

'Any Superquinn sausages left?' She smiled at him.

'They're cooking right as we speak. Is your . . . er . . . date with you?' He looked out over her shoulder.

'No . . . I left him sitting in a Russian restaurant. It's not every day I get invited to a fry-up.'

'It's not everyone gets invited to one either, I'll have you know,' he joked, standing back to let her in.

'Howya, Alison? Ye made it after all.' Fintan stood up politely as she entered.

'Hiya, Fintan. Yeah, the lure of a real fry-up got the better of me.'

'How's it goin', Alison? Would ye like a pint or a glass of wine?' Frankie stuck his head out the kitchen door. He had a tea towel slung over his shoulder.

'Frankie's on cooks. He's a class act at doing a fry,' JJ explained, as she handed him her coat.

Fintan gave a wolf whistle when he saw the simple black backless dress she wore.

Alison laughed. 'Where's your wife tonight?' she asked, feeling quite at home.

'It's her book-club night, and the kids are staying at their cousins', one of them had a birthday party.' Fintan raised his beer glass.

'So what are ye having then?' Frankie cocked an eyebrow at her. He had the kindest hazel eyes. His wife had recently had their first child.

'Any chance of a cuppa?' she asked, easing her feet out of her stilettos.

'I'll make you one. Milk no sugar?' JJ offered straight away.

'Absolutely *no* sugar,' she replied emphatically.

'You're a real little titch out of them shoes. How do ye wimmen sthand in them?' Fintan studied her heels in some bemusement.

'A woman's gotta do what a woman's gotta do, Fintan,' she said seriously, and giggled at the expression on his face.

She hadn't laughed so much in a long time, she reflected several hours later, as the two F's made ready to leave. After they had tucked into rashers, sausages, pudding, eggs, mushrooms and fried potatoes and mugs of Barry's tea, they'd cleared the table and played several riotous games of Sevens. Alison hadn't played cards since her childhood, but it came back to her, and she won a couple of games, with much slagging and teasing from the others.

'Go down those stairs quietly,' JJ warned. 'I'm in fear of my life of another visit from Mrs W.'

'Ah go on, I think you fancy her,' Alison jeered.

'I do, yeah – she's all I dream about,' JJ retorted, as his friends bade whispered goodnights and went quietly down the stairs.

'I better go too,' she said regretfully. 'I'm going home for my mother's surprise seventieth birthday party and I haven't even packed yet. That's one of the reasons I steered clear of the wine.'

'What time's your flight?' JJ closed the door gently.

'It's the Aer Lingus flight from JFK tomorrow afternoon.'

'Is your boyfriend bringing you?'

'Nope,' she said emphatically.

'*Is* he your boyfriend?' JJ looked at her quizzically.

'Well, we weren't exclusive.' She shrugged.

'Tsk! That non-exclusive nonsense makes no sense to me. Either you're going with someone or you're not,' JJ snorted. 'I have no truck with it at all. If I'm dating a woman, I'm dating her and I expect her to be dating me.'

I see,' she said mildly. 'And *are* you dating a woman, exclusively or non-exclusively?'

'No, the last woman I dated was a bad loser at cards.' His eyes were glinting with amusement.

'Smarty,' she retorted. 'I'm off. I need to get my beauty sleep.'

'Did you not have your afternoon nap?' he said slyly.

'You're very funny, aren't you?' She grabbed her shoes.

'I'll give you a lift to JFK tomorrow,' he offered.

'Oh God no, I wouldn't put you to the trouble, JJ. I'll get a taxi,' she said firmly.

'Ah whist, woman, I might need a favour from you some time. That's what good neighbours are for.' He stood with his arms folded, having none of it.

'No, honestly!'

'Be ready at twelve,' he ordered.

'There you go, bossing me around again.'

'It's therapy for me. I had a terrible childhood with the three older sisters I was telling you about.'

Alison giggled. 'You're incorrigible. Goodnight.'

'That's a big word for the likes of me, Dunwoody. Goodnight, and thanks for coming.'

'Thanks for the invite.' Their eyes met and they smiled at each other, and then she slipped past him and went barefoot down the stairs, the third step creaking as it always did. It was a sound she was now becoming quite familiar with.

Chapter 8

'So are you looking forward to your trip home?' JJ asked, tapping his fingers rhythmically on the steering wheel as they sat in heavy traffic en route to JFK. Alison turned back to face him; she had turned to look behind her as the iconic skyline of Manhattan grew further away and they crossed the river to Queens.

'I'm really looking forward to seeing my parents and sister and her kids. I just can't believe that my mam is seventy. And I'm dying to see her face when she sees me, but part of me wants to be here to try and get a job. I really took a hammering, JJ, when the firm collapsed. I've worked my ass off and I had a good lifestyle, savings and investments, and it's nearly all gone. I've very little left to show for years of study, years of hard graft, so I feel I've no business gadding off home. But of course I can't say that to my sister – she'd have a fit. She doesn't know I've lost my job, and I don't want them to know at the moment anyway. I don't want to spoil my mother's party. I can't make up my mind whether to stay until Christmas or not.'

'That's rough, not being able to tell people, but try and enjoy your time at home. And *stay* for Christmas. Come back in the New Year refreshed and ready to go,' he advised.

'Yeah, perhaps you're right, but when your cash is dwindling away it's kinda scary. I went out with some friends at the weekend, and two of us had lost our jobs, and it was so strange looking for the cheapest thing on the menu and just having one drink – not that I'm an alcoholic or anything,' she said hastily.

'I know what you mean: basically, counting your pennies when before you didn't give it a thought. At least you don't have a mortgage or kids to support,' he pointed out.

'That would be the pits,' she agreed.

'Maybe you could become a card shark.' He grinned. 'You showed great potential last night. It was a laugh, wasn't it?'

'Yeah, I haven't played cards in *years*. It's a real Irish thing.'

'Next time there's a fry-up and a card night I'll be sure to let you know,' he promised, as the Manhattan skyline became a blur in the distance.

They sat in silence, lost in their own thoughts for a while. Although he'd chatted affably with her, Alison felt JJ was a little distracted. She hoped he wasn't regretting his offer to give her a lift. It was a chunk of time out of his working day – something she'd think twice about doing if she'd been in gainful employment, she thought wryly.

She sighed again. She had such ambivalent feelings about going home. She was longing to see everyone, of course, but her circumstances were far from ideal. Maybe JJ was feeling sorry for her, feeling pity that she couldn't afford the taxi ride. How mortifying was that? she thought, cringing inwardly, totally sorry that she'd accepted his offer of a lift to the airport. She should have done as she always did . . . stood on her own two feet. It was the best way, then you were obligated to no one, Alison thought grimly, staring unseeingly out the window.

What daft impulse had made him offer to drive Alison to JFK, JJ thought irritably, slowing to under twenty as the traffic increased as they got closer to the airport. What was he doing, flirting and bantering with her and inviting her up to his place for fry-ups? It seemed like such a betrayal of his wife. He banished the thought instantly. He wasn't going down that route. That only led to feelings of guilt. He had enough to deal with, he thought angrily as he heard the woman beside him sigh deeply. She had her own problems, he acknowledged. Losing her job and her apartment and having nothing on the horizon was a daunting situation for sure. Going home under such circumstances was tough. It had been a neighbourly gesture to offer her a lift. But if that was all it was, why did he feel so bloody guilty?

'Thanks so much for the lift, JJ,' Alison said politely as he pulled up at the set-down area.

'I'll get you again, don't worry,' he promised her, opening the door to get her case from the boot.

'It can't possibly be as cold at home as it is here.' She shivered, pulling the collar of her woollen coat up over her ears.

'It's bad enough I heard. I was talking to my mother last night and she said it was arctic,' JJ remarked, as he lifted the case out of the boot as if it were a feather and clicked open the wheels for her.

'Thanks JJ, have a great Christmas. I'll see you after the holidays,' she said warmly, feeling kindly towards him again.

'Will do, and the same to you,' he said, and turned to get back in the car. She took hold of her case and began to move towards the entrance when she heard him call her name.

'Alison!'

'Yes?' She turned to look back at him. He had a serious, intent look on his face that surprised her. 'Could you just give me five minutes in the car? I . . . I need to talk to you about something,' he asked quietly.

'Sure,' she agreed, flabbergasted. What on earth was he going to say to her? What did he need to talk about? He hefted the case into the rear of the car and she climbed back in.

'What's the problem?' She came straight out with it, turning to face him.

'Remember when I told you I was married and had no kids?' he said flatly.

'Yeah,' she said slowly, her heart beginning to thud against her ribs. *Oh God, please, please don't let him say he's married or seeing someone, let him be one of the good guys*, Alison prayed silently.

'My wife died four years ago. She was killed in a car crash by a drunken driver. We were married just over a year.' His blue eyes were dark with the pain of loss and remembrance.

'Oh JJ!' she whispered, stunned. 'I'm so, so sorry. I don't know what to say.'

'It's OK. You don't have to say anything. I don't really talk about it much. It was why I came to America, to try and put it behind me. That's why I always go home at Christmas. To see my folks and to visit the grave.'

'Thanks for telling me.' She reached out and touched his arm. She would have liked to hug him but didn't want to seem pushy. He might not welcome it.

'As I say, I don't really talk about it, but all my friends know, of course, and I wanted to let you know the score, seeing as now you're one of them.' He gave a crooked little smile.

'I'm glad we're friends,' she managed.

'That's good to know.' He sat staring at her, his hands gripping the steering wheel, exuding an air of sadness that cut her to the quick.

'Just because we're friends doesn't mean you can get away with bossing me around all the time.' She swallowed, trying not to burst into tears, not knowing what to say.

'Arrah, a bit of bossing will do you all the good in the world, my dear good woman.' He smiled at her, and she knew instinctively that he had taken a step forward by telling her of his tragedy, and drawing her into his circle of friends. She felt incredibly touched that he had felt he could be so honest with her.

'So when do you come home?' she asked.

'Next Wednesday. I like to spend some time with my folks – they're getting on. I'll be up in Dublin for a day before I go back. In fact, I fly out of Dublin. One of my sisters lives in Skerries. Her baby's due, so she won't be travelling to the West. Maybe we could link up for a drink?' He looked her straight in the eye.

'Is that one of the sisters that gave you the traumatic childhood?' she said to lighten the moment and make it easier for him.

'She was the worst,' he said, the old familiar twinkle creeping back into his eyes.

'I guess I better meet up with you so, so you can have a bit of therapy bossing me around, to get you back on an even keel, so to speak,' she retorted, searching in her bag for a pen. She wrote two telephone numbers down on the back of her business card. 'Home and cell,' she said, handing it to him.

'Right. I'll be in touch,' he promised, slipping it into his jeans pocket.

'I better go,' she said. 'See you at home then.'

'That will be nice. Thanks for being kind.' He met her gaze. 'It's hard to move on, you know what I'm saying . . .' he said awkwardly.

'I'm sure it is, JJ. I couldn't begin to imagine what you've been through. I hope it gets easier in time,' she said gently.

'It's always hard going home. It always brings it back. A lot of the time I can put it aside here, but Christmas is difficult.'

'I'm sure it is,' she agreed as he opened the car door and removed her case again and carried it to the kerb for her.

'Safe journey, Alison,' he said quietly. 'Enjoy your mam's party.'

'I will,' she said. 'Take care of yourself, JJ.'

'Don't forget to take your nap in the afternoon, Dunwoody,' he teased, and she laughed, glad he was making an effort and showing his old spark.

She reached up and gave him a peck on the cheek. 'My dear good man, you're pushing your luck, get outta here before I turn *really* nasty.'

He gave her a quick hug and then he was sliding his long legs into his jeep, and she felt inexplicably lonely as he beeped at her and drove away.

What an absolute tragedy to have befallen him. Except for aunts, she'd never been touched by the loss of a close family member, and it was something she shied away from thinking about. She'd been very close to her father's sister in particular, and had been shocked at the finality of death. She did believe in life after death, but she never wanted to be parted from her loved ones. The thought of not having her mother and dad and Olivia and her family, and Uncle Leo, was unbearable.

How did JJ manage to appear so good-humoured? How did he put one foot in front of the other each day? Time had obviously eased his mourning somewhat, but even so a loss like that was not borne easily, and there had been deep pain and sorrow mirrored in his eyes when he'd spoken of his wife's death.

She went through the chore of checking in and going through Security, glad to have her mind occupied. His disclosure had rattled her; she couldn't stop thinking of that look of sadness. Part of her wished he hadn't told her. Their relationship was no longer on a level playing field. The shadow of his dead wife would hover over it, and whereas before his revelation she'd been happy enough to go with the flow of it, now she felt constrained. He'd told her he was finding it hard to move on. Was that a subtle hint that he didn't want her getting any ideas about a future relationship? And *had* she been thinking in these terms – even subconsciously? Typical of her luck, Alison thought crossly, putting the thought out of her head. There was no point in going there consciously or bloody subconsciously. He'd practically told her in no uncertain terms that he wasn't interested in anything more than friendship, so she'd have to deal with it and get over herself. She was putting him firmly out of her head, Alison decided. She had enough to deal with going home as it was, without added complications.

It was a relief finally to board the big green and white airbus, and Alison's heart lifted when she saw the familiar green shamrock and heard the soft Cork lilt of the air hostess as she welcomed her aboard. Excitement and anticipation surged through her. Soon she'd feel her mother and father's arms around her. How wonderful that would be. How lucky she was to have them, Alison thought gratefully as she stowed her hand luggage and sank into her premium seat. She always flew with the Irish airline when she was going back to Ireland. She didn't care who she flew with when she was going stateside. But getting on to that Aer Lingus plane was always one of the best parts of coming home.

'OK, hon, I'm off. Should be back by ten. I'll ring you when I come off the M1, and you can meet us at Mam's.' Olivia gave her husband a kiss, grabbed her car keys and hurried out of the house, shivering in the damp cold of the early morning. It was raining, and the windows of her small Fiesta were fogged up. She cursed as she wiped the front one, too impatient to wait for the heater to clear them. She was running late, but at least there wouldn't be the usual rush hour on a Saturday morning. She had texted '**Welcome Home**' to Alison's mobile so she'd know that her sister had landed when she got the delivery-report message. The flight was on time: she'd checked the teletext and she wanted to be there when Alison came through.

When Alison had phoned from JFK to say that she was boarding, Olivia had let on that she wouldn't be at the airport, saying that something had come up and Michael wouldn't be free to mind the kids so Alison would have to get a taxi. 'No worries,' Alison had said cheerily. 'Can't wait to see everyone.'

Now that the day of the party had arrived, Olivia had stopped worrying. Today was all about their mother, she'd decided. Alison would provide an extra pair of hands after she'd had a few hours' sleep.

The children, of course, knew nothing of her visit or of the surprise party. It had been hard enough keeping the secret herself, she thought as she left the village and headed for the motorway. The traffic was light, and she got to the airport in good time. She had to park in the Outer Siberia that was Block C, and she heard her phone beep and knew that it was the message report that told her her sister had landed and was possibly even disembarked. Olivia drove around like a madwoman looking for a parking spot and had to drive up to level three before she found one. By the time she got to Arrivals, she was panting after racing along the dank, dimly lit car parks, nearly going on her ear on a patch of oil at one stage.

'Oh God, I need to get fit,' she muttered, as she scanned the board to see that the flight had landed on time. She studied the people emerging through Customs, wondering if they were from the New York flight. The big giveaway would be the groups of women who had gone on their Christmas-shopping expedition. Some of the passengers emerging had tans, she noted, so no, perhaps not.

She was gasping for a cup of coffee, but she was afraid to leave in case Alison came out when she was gone. More passengers came through, and then there was a lull and then one or two stragglers. Maybe she would risk running over to the coffee bar, she dithered. The doors opened again, and women pushing trolleys piled high with cases surged through. It had to be the New York flight, she guessed, as one woman, yawning her head off, struggled to keep control of her laden trolley. Olivia scanned the hordes that kept on surging forward. And then she saw a familiar auburn head, and her sister, looking a million dollars in an expensive-looking black wool coat and a lilac scarf knotted casually at her neck, appeared, not bothering to look at the group of greeters huddled at the rail, but focusing on the exit where the taxi rank was.

Olivia, delighted to see her, forgot all her irritations and resentments towards her younger sister and called her name. Her sister didn't hear her. 'Alison, Alison,' she called loudly again, and Alison looked in Olivia's direction and then came the heartwarming moment of delighted recognition as she left her trolley in the middle of the concourse and raced into her sister's welcoming arms.

'Oh, you brat, I thought there wasn't going to be anyone here,' she remonstrated, as they hugged the daylights out of each other.

'Ah, just wanted to give you a surprise. You look great for someone who's just flown through the night.' Olivia took her arm and went to rescue the trolley.

'Oh Lord, I'm knackered, but I'm dying to see Mam and Dad and Michael and the girls.' Alison sighed happily.

'Well, it will be a while, I had to park in Block C. It took me as long to get parking as it did to get here.' Olivia took charge of the trolley and led the way to the pay machines. 'That's a fabulous coat. I suppose it cost an arm and a leg – it looks it – and so does the bag,' she said enviously, running her hand along the soft forearm of Alison's coat.

'Er . . . yeah, it was expensive all right,' Alison agreed.

'How wonderful to be able to buy clothes without feeling a scintilla of guilt. The nearest thing I get to a designer bag is buying a fake at the market,' confessed Olivia, feeding a ten-euro note into the machine.

I couldn't even afford that at the moment. Alison scowled, feeling a surge of resentment towards her sister for making her feel guilty. Olivia was so good at pressing her guilt buttons and always had been. Did all older sisters do it, or just hers? She was sorely tempted to tell her *exactly* what was going on in her life, but pride held her back. Even though she felt a complete failure, she didn't want her family to know that she *was* one. Not on her first day home.

'I have Mam's bracelet in my bag – it's wrapped beautifully. I love the Tiffany colours.' Alison swallowed her resentment and changed the subject as they eventually settled into the car after their long trudge from Arrivals.

'Great, she'll be able to wear it tonight. She has absolutely no idea,' Olivia said, as she started up the engine, unaware of her younger sister's angst. 'The flowers have to be collected and arranged. And the room just needs to be decorated a little bit. I thought some wide cream candles and poinsettias would be nice.'

'If we could get some holly and ivy we could twine it along the windowsills,' Alison suggested.

'Oh, thank God you're here, you were always good at that kind of stuff,' Olivia exclaimed. 'I'll send Michael out to get some, there's a big holly bush in the church grounds, and we have ivy on the wall at the end of the garden.'

'Great stuff.' Alison yawned.

'We'll go and see Mam and Dad and have a bit of breakfast with them and then you can go and have a snooze and I'll give you a shout around half-two – how's that?' Olivia proposed.

'Perfect,' said her sister. 'Just perfect.'

Chapter 9

'Remember when it was a windy country road home?' Alison said as Olivia indicated to come off the motorway and took the slip road to Port Ross.

'It takes no time now, unless you get stuck in the rush hour,' her sister remarked, slowing down to keep within the speed limit. She'd phoned Michael on her hands-free to tell him to meet her with the girls at Esther and Liam's house.

'I think it's a better idea to surprise Mam at home rather than at the party, don't you?' Alison said thoughtfully.

'Absolutely. You know Mam, she's such a softie she'll be in tears when she sees you and, besides, she'll have two surprises today. You this morning and the party tonight.

And, anyway, she'll have more time to enjoy her . . . her joy, knowing that you're here, if you know what I mean.' Olivia whizzed past a pothole with a sudden swerve of the wheel. 'Bloody roads,' she muttered.

'That was here the last time I was here. Melora and I were driving along and I nearly decapitated her because I never saw it.' Alison smiled at the memory. Her friend had phoned to wish her well and to tell her that she was playing volleyball on Venice Beach and had two interviews lined up.

'How is Melora?' asked Olivia.

'She's in LA looking for a job,' Alison said, without thinking.

'She's leaving New York? I thought she really liked it there,' her sister said in surprise.

'Oh . . . oh . . . she does, she did . . . er . . . She met a guy. You know Melora – she's mad keen to get married,' Alison rallied, determined to keep the news of her changed circumstances a secret.

'Tell her to stay single. Believe me, you never have one second to yourself when you have a husband and children,' Olivia retorted.

'But you're happy, aren't you?' Alison looked at her sister, surprised by the vehemence of her response.

'I suppose I am, but it's a bit wearing looking after my lot, holding down a job, and minding the parents and Uncle Leo. Being single has a lot going for it.'

'Oh!' murmured Alison. She felt Olivia had thrown a barb. She often told Alison that she had a charmed life, but no one had *begged* Olivia to get married and have children or to stay at home in Port Ross, that was *her* choice, thought Alison resentfully. If Olivia knew how things *really* were with Alison right now, she might not be so quick to whinge to her.

'Ah, don't mind me,' Olivia said, a bit shamefaced, after a few moments of silence. 'I've just been worrying about the party, wanting to be sure it will turn out OK. I'm really glad you're here, it takes the pressure off.'

'It's only a party, and it's only family. If things go wrong, they go wrong, and nothing's going to go wrong, I'm sure – and if it does we'll sort it,' Alison said reassuringly, realizing that her older sister had been under a lot of pressure.

'I know we will.' Olivia smiled at her. 'Frig it, whatever happens, let's enjoy it, we're lucky to have Mam and Dad still with us to celebrate.'

Two minutes later they turned a bend and came on to the coast road. 'Oh, look at the sea. Isn't it fabulous?' Alison rolled down her window and inhaled deep lungfuls of salty air. The waves were tumultuous, grey-green whitecaps crashing against the shore. 'Oh, it's good to be home,' she exclaimed, as some of the stresses and strains of the past few weeks seemed to lift and float away far out to sea. JJ was right: she should rest and relax and go back to New York ready for action in the New Year.

'I've an idea,' she said impulsively as they drove through the village towards their parents' house. 'Why don't I stay in the car, and when you go inside I'll ring and pretend I'm in New York – but you pick up because my Irish number will come up on Mam's caller ID. And then I'll knock on the door.'

'*Brilliant* idea!' Olivia enthused, eyes gleaming with anticipation.

Her sister looked tired, and the lines around her mouth and eyes had deepened, Alison noted with a dart of dismay. The first telltale signs of middle age were making their appearance. There was a smattering of alarming grey hairs in her sister's chestnut bob, and dark circles under her eyes.

Olivia was forty now, incredible as it was, Alison reminded herself as they drove through the quiet fishing village where they'd grown up. Two women in rain macs walked into the butcher's, and an elderly man struggled to let his umbrella down before entering Nolan's to get his paper. A couple sat in the small coffee shop having breakfast. Otherwise, the street was deserted on that wet, windy Saturday morning. They passed the road that led to the pier where fishing boats rocked up and down on the waves and seagulls hawked and squawked, circling a small trawler that was unloading its catch. A green fishing net, caught against a bollard, flapped in the wind. The rigging in the masts of the boats jangled, making its own music, and the wood in the trawlers creaked and groaned as they rocked against the quay. It was the sound of home, thought Alison, as memories came flooding back,

The house looked as she always remembered it: an ivy-clad dormer bungalow with neatly clipped privet, a weeping willow in the centre of the garden and polyanthus and pansies in the well-tended flowerbeds under the windows making a defiantly colourful stand against the gloomy backdrop of bad weather.

Two cars sat on the tarmacadamed drive, and she knew the maroon Passat behind her parents' Volkswagen was her brother-in-law's. Olivia parked on the street. 'Give me two minutes and then ring,' she grinned, getting out of the car. Alison watched her hurry up the drive, the wind blowing her hood off her head. She was dying to see her parents, longing for their hugs. She waited the two minutes and rang the number.

'Hello?' Olivia pretended innocence.

'Hi,' murmured Alison.

'Oh! *Alison*, you'd think we planned it! We were just going to sing "Happy Birthday" to Mam. Hold on until I give her the phone and you can join in. I'll put you on speaker.' Olivia played her part to perfection, with just the right amount of surprise. Alison could hear the chatter of the children in the background.

'Hello, pet, you're up early,' her mother said, the speaker giving a tinny effect to the call.

'I set my clock. I wanted to wish you happy birthday, Mam.'

'Aren't you the darling,' her mother said, and Alison just knew she had tears in her eyes.

'Let's all sing,' Olivia commanded.

There was a chorus of 'Happy Birthday to you,' and Alison joined in with gusto, glad no one was walking along the road to see her singing her head off into a cell phone.

'I wish I was there with you all.' Alison injected a note of sadness in her tone when it was over. She was even better at this acting lark than Olivia, she thought smugly.

'I wish you were here too. Isn't there *any* chance of you getting home this Christmas?' Esther asked plaintively.

'Not a hope with the way things are going. But look, Mam, have a great day and enjoy your meal tonight with the family. And raise a glass for me,' she added poignantly, for good measure.

'I will, pet, I will, but it won't be the same without you. Say hello to your father.' Esther was definitely teary at this stage, and Alison began to feel a bit mean.

'Hello, Dad, it sounds like a madhouse there.'

'It is a bit,' her father said mildly. 'How are you?'

'Great, great. Looking forward to a lie-in seeing as I don't have to get up today,' – that wasn't a lie: she *was* longing for sleep, she thought as the weariness of jet lag hit her in a wave of tiredness.

'You enjoy it and take it easy, you work too hard,' her father declared.

Not any more, she was tempted to say, but she held it back, she wasn't going to spoil her mother's birthday with her tale of gloom and doom. 'Not a bit of it, Dad. Have a good day today. God bless,' she said, suddenly anxious to be inside with them.

'Bye, love,' he said.

'Bye, everyone, and happy birthday, Mam,' said Alison and heard a chorus of goodbyes before she hung up. She tucked her phone in her bag and got out of the car, racing up the path as quick as she could, filled with eager anticipation. She took a deep breath and scrambled for her keys in her cavernous bag. The set of keys to her parents' house was on her keyring. She found them and slid the key in the lock, and gently opened the door. She stood in the hall and inhaled the familiar scent of home. A vase of winter roses stood on the hall table and the scent from a fragrance diffuser with long, narrow, scented sticks mingled with the smell of wax polish and baking. She could hear the buzz of conversation and excited children's chatter in the kitchen.

Alison pushed open the door. Her mother was sitting at the table in her dressing gown, surrounded by her three grandchildren, who were helping her to unwrap presents. She looked pale and older than Alison remembered, she thought with a shock. That flu had taken its toll. Her father had his back to her as he reached into the fridge for milk. Olivia smiled, and Michael, her brother-in-law, winked.

'Happy Birthday, Mam,' said Alison quietly, as a lump the size of a golf ball rose in her throat.

Esther looked up, stunned. 'Alison! Oh, Alison darling,' she exclaimed joyously, jumping up from her chair and, arms outstretched, she gathered her daughter to enfold her in the most welcome hug Alison had ever had in her life. Then it was her father's turn, and she leaned her head against his shoulder and felt safe and protected like she used to when she was a little girl. Here, in the fortification of her childhood home, it didn't seem to matter that she was jobless and had lost most of what she'd worked for. Here were security and love, and a sense that everything would be all right.

'Auntie Alison, Auntie Alison.' It was the twins' turn next to launch themselves at her. Ellie stood back, unsure. It was eighteen months since Alison had seen her, and she couldn't get over the size of her.

'Well, aren't you the little rip, pretending to ring me from America?' Her mother was laughing and crying at the same time.

'Good, wasn't it?' Alison smirked, kissing Esther again over the top of her nieces' heads.

'How long are you staying? I'll have to air your room. I can't believe you're here.' Her mother was in a tizzy.

'Calm down, Mam,' Olivia interjected. 'I'll sort the room later. Alison's staying with me tonight. She can come home tomorrow.'

'When do you go back, I suppose it's a flying visit?' Esther sighed, holding Alison's hand tightly.

'Actually I'm not going back until after Christmas—'

'You're here for Christmas?' Esther was gobsmacked. 'Why, what's wrong?'

Olivia's jaw dropped.

Alison stood there as they all looked at her, astonished. It would be so easy to tell them she was jobless and on the skids and just get it out of the way, it would be a huge relief, she thought wearily. But how could she do it on her mother's birthday and ruin the lovely surprise she'd just given her? How selfish would that be? And then she'd have to endure all the questions, and word would leak out to the neighbours and relations, and she just couldn't bear the thought of their pity and, in the case of two of her cousins who weren't great fans of hers, their smug delight at her fall. No, this wasn't the time or the place to make her revelation.

'Nothing's wrong,' she said calmly, privately marvelling at her mother's astuteness. 'I just wanted to come home for Christmas. It's been a while.'

'Hurray!!' Kate yelled, punching the air.

'That's great news altogether,' her father exclaimed.

'I had leave to take, so when I was coming home for the pa— to see you,' she corrected herself hastily when Olivia flashed her a look of consternation, 'I decided I'd take it. I haven't been home for Christmas in ages.' She was turning into the most accomplished liar, she acknowledged wryly.

'This is the best birthday present I could ever have had.' Esther had tears running down her cheeks.

'Don't cry, Mam, stop.' Alison threw her eyes up to heaven and glanced over at Olivia, who seemed just as stunned at the news. Esther wiped her eyes.

'Why are you crying, Gran? Are you very sad?'
Ellie threw her little arms around her grandmother.

'I'm crying because I'm happy. I'm the luckiest woman in the world to have all my family around me on my birthday.'

'And we're having a Chinese tonight in the restaurant. We're getting dressed up,' Lia informed Alison. 'Will you be coming?'

'I certainly will.' Alison hugged her, marvelling at how pretty she was with her blond hair tied in two pigtails and her fringe feathering her big blue eyes.

'Brill,' said her niece. 'Can I have some lipstick?'

'If your Mam lets you.' Alison nodded.

'Can I, Mam? Can I?' Lia demanded.

'Cam, I?' said Ellie, tugging at Alison's arm.

Alison looked at Olivia for confirmation. 'Go on, this once,' she said.

'Cool,' said Lia with satisfaction. She loved when her aunt was home. Alison had brilliant high heels and let them use her make-up to dress up.

'I hope they give us that big round table with the thing in the middle that makes the food go around.' Kate draped an arm around her grandmother's shoulder as she sat down at the table again.

'That's the one I asked for,' Olivia said, giving Alison the tiniest wink as she filled the kettle and switched it on to make the tea.

'Did you bring us some presents?' Ellie fixed her aunt with a blue-eyed stare.

'Ellie! That's rude,' hissed Lia.

'Yes, Ellie, you don't ask people for presents,' Olivia said sternly.

'Sorry.' Ellie's lip wobbled.

'Of course I have presents for you, darling.' Alison knelt down beside her and put her arm around her. 'I've Hershey bars in my bag for you as well. Can I give them one?' She cocked an eye at her sister as the children's eyes lit up at this unexpected treat.

'Oh go on,' sighed Olivia. 'Chocolate bars for breakfast! What next?'

'It *is* a very special occasion,' Kate pointed out earnestly.

'I can't argue with that.' Olivia smiled, amused in spite of herself.

'Give me your coat, Alison,' her brother-in-law said after she'd distributed the eagerly received bars, 'and sit down and take the weight off your feet.'

'I will,' Alison said gratefully, shrugging out of her coat and loosening her scarf and handing them to him. He hung them in the small hall between the kitchen and utility room. She walked around the table to where Olivia was standing and stood beside her sister. 'Are we giving Mam our prezzie now or, or . . .' She'd been about to say 'at the party' but had managed to stop herself before blurting it out. Alison was beginning to understand the pressure Olivia had spoken of earlier of everything going OK for the party and not letting the cat out of the bag. She'd nearly let it slip and she was only home ten minutes. 'Or will we wait until the meal tonight?' she amended.

'Ah, you can't do that,' protested Esther. 'That would be cruel to make me wait until tonight, wouldn't it, girls?' she appealed to her grandchildren.

'Patience is a virtue,' Lia said primly, in exactly the same tone as her mother would use.

'Lia Hammond!' Esther spluttered.

'Only joking, Gran.' Lia exploded into the most infectious giggle.

'I agree with Lia. It will give you something to look forward to,' Liam teased, knowing how his wife was like a child where presents were concerned and was always trying to find out what he'd bought her for Christmas and birthdays. This year he'd given her a weekend away at a luxury hotel and spa. His wife *adored* such treats.

'Don't be such a meanie, you. Come on, girls; don't keep your poor old mother in suspense,' Esther begged.

'If you guess what it is, we'll give it to you.' Olivia grinned at her.

'Ah no! Don't do that to me.' Esther groaned.

'Don't be mean, let's give it to her now.' Alison kissed the top of her mother's head again and wrapped her arms around her.

'It's good to have one pal.' Esther stroked her cheek tenderly.

'Now! Now! Now!' Kate banged on the table with her teaspoon.

'Yes! Yes! Yes!' chanted Lia, doing a twirl.

'All right then,' relented Olivia. 'It's a very special one for a very special mother, all the way from New York. We chose it together on the internet and Alison got it,' she explained, as her sister rooted in her bag for the box.

'You give it, seeing as you're the oldest,' Alison grinned, handing Olivia the Tiffany package.

'Mam, from the two of us with love.' Olivia kissed her mother as she handed her the present.

'Oh my goodness! What's this? Oh my God! *Tiffany's* – how posh!' Esther exclaimed excitedly as the grandchildren crowded around her for a look.

'Open it, open it,' Kate urged.

'Oh, girls!' Esther exclaimed as she opened the beautifully wrapped box. 'Oh my Lord, this is beautiful.' She held up the diamond-encrusted bangle and slipped it on to her wrist, twisting it this way and that as the children oohed and aahed.

'You can wear it tonight to the—' Olivia gave her a dig in the ribs. 'To . . . to the meal out,' Alison stuttered, aghast that she'd nearly let it slip again.

'*You* must be hungry, love,' Liam interjected. 'Sit down there and I'll cook you some breakfast.'

'Is there any of Mam's homemade brown bread?' Alison asked wistfully. 'I'd love a slice of that. I couldn't eat a fry. I'm too excited to be home.'

'There's a fresh loaf and a currant loaf and plenty of scones.' Esther couldn't take her eyes off her gift.

'Cam we have some?' piped up Ellie, and her mother darted her a glare. Olivia was constantly warning the children not to be asking for food at their Gran's, to absolutely no avail.

'Of course you can, pet.' Esther laughed at the hopeful anticipation in her grandchild's voice.

'A feast,' Alison declared as the doorbell rang.

'Who would that be on a wet Saturday morning?' Esther wondered.

'I'll get it.' Alison, who was nearest the door, stood up.

She knew when she saw the stooped outline and the shape of a hat through the frosted glass of the front door exactly who it was.

'Uncle Leo!' She beamed with pleasure when she opened the door to find him standing in the porch with a small tree in a container.

'It's yourself! Ah, lassie, you're a treat for sore eyes.' Her uncle's face lit up and he gave her a big bear hug, knocking his hat off in the process. 'When did you get home?'

'About an hour ago.' She smiled as she stepped back to let him in.

'Let me get the present for Esther.' He bent with difficulty to pick up the container, and she felt a pang of dismay as she saw how stiff he was. It was the first time she'd ever really noticed that both her parents were getting on in years and that it was starting to show. Now Leo was leaning heavily on his stick as he limped into the kitchen. Suddenly she was glad she was home for Christmas. She'd forgotten how important family was, she thought guiltily, remembering her trips to Aspen and the Caribbean the previous two years. Olivia really did mind them all, she thought, remembering vaguely her sister's last email about having to bring Leo for some breathing test.

'Happy Birthday, Esther.' Leo thrust the container at his sister-in-law. 'It's an acer, a Japanese maple, I know you're fond of them. It's a very fine specimen, I got good advice from a gardener chap I know. In fact he got it for me, and it's the best that could be got.'

'Ah Leo, you're very thoughtful,' Esther said, touched. 'Thank you so much. Come in and sit down and have a cup of tea and a scone. Michael, would you take the tree off Leo and put it in the back?' She smiled at her son-in-law.

'You're welcome, and thanks for the offer of the tea. I see the gang's all here.' He rubbed his hands in delight as the twins flung themselves at him.

'Uncle Leo, will you play sword fights with us with your walking stick?' Kate begged. It was one of their favourite games. 'Please, Uncle Leo,' Lia urged, clasping her hands together in supplication.

'After we've had the tea,' Olivia ordered, bringing the pot to the table. Liam placed a basket of scones and a plate of sliced currant and brown bread on the table.

'I'll get the jam and marmalade.' Alison went to the cupboard.

'And get the butter while you're at it,' Esther reminded her, 'and don't forget the jam spoon.'

Alison smiled to herself. Esther was a stickler for not allowing buttery knives into the jam and marmalade and had always insisted on them using jam spoons. Neither would she allow a carton of milk on the table. Milk was always poured from a jug.

She turned from the fridge and took in the scene before her. Ellie was sitting on Esther's lap looking at her birthday cards. Liam was putting knives and plates on the table, Olivia was pouring the tea, Michael was pouring a cup of milk for Ellie, the twins sat on either side of Uncle Leo telling him about a 'real' fight in the schoolyard. The kitchen was snug and warm as the rain hammered on the windows. She exhaled as tension seeped away. Coming home was the best thing she could have done for herself after the battering her confidence and finances had taken.

And, although she'd never really understood it or acknowledged it before, her coming home was a joyful thing for her family. It was a closing of the circle, and the falling economy and gloom and doom of the recession could make no dent in it, or prevail against that powerful force of energy that a united family gives. She might have lost material wealth and possessions, but she was enriched beyond measure by all the love, joy and goodwill that was in this homely kitchen right now. Family was all that mattered at the end of the day, Alison acknowledged gladly as she went to join her loved ones at the table.

Chapter 10

'Oh, you've done a great job of the room, Alison. Well done!' Olivia exclaimed later that afternoon as she stood beside her sister and gazed around the private room of the Golden Dragon. The rectangular table at the top where the family were to be seated looked on to several circular tables, where the guests would sit. Alison had fashioned small wreaths of holly, ivy, evergreen and yellow roses on every table. In the centre of each wreath three votive candles in small glass holders were ready to be lit.

An artful display of massed poinsettias and cream candles stood on top of a gleaming mahogany sideboard, where champagne glasses on trays stood waiting for their fizzy sparkling liquid. The two windowsills were draped with greenery, with red and gold ribbons entwined through the branches matching the red gold-flock paper on the walls. It was very tastefully done and gave the room a touch of class. It was almost dark outside, and the small red lamps dotted along the walls poured soft light into the room, giving a cosy, intimate ambiance.

'Glad you like it,' Alison said, pleased with the effect herself. 'What else do you want me to do?'

'Umm, we have the cake, and the music is sorted. And champagne will be served as the guests come in; the glasses are ready. I think we have everything covered.' Olivia bit her thumb nail in concentration.

'And you're sure about place names?' Alison said.

'Let them sit where they want. That way the ones that don't get on don't have to end up sitting beside each other,' Olivia said firmly.

'Pity we had to ask Bert and Tessa and those two obnoxious sons of theirs.' Alison frowned.

'They're Dad and Leo's family, and you know Mam would have been upset if we hadn't. You know what she's like for doing the right thing.'

'Indeed I do,' said Alison, with a heartfelt sigh, and Olivia laughed.

'I hate the way they just assume they're going to get Leo's land and they never even bother their fat backsides to help him out. One day I went over and he was trying to sweep out the yard, and he's not able for it any more. Michael went over and did it the next day for him, but that pair wouldn't even call to see if he's alive.' Olivia grimaced.

'You see, if we did place names we could put them beside Mrs Harney . . .' Alison said wickedly.

'Don't tempt me.' Olivia laughed. Mrs Harney was an elderly widow who lived alone. She was a close neighbour, and Esther was always very kind to her. She could be brusque at times and never held back if she had something to say. She didn't mix much with people in the village, but she liked Esther and welcomed their chats. Olivia had invited her knowing that Mrs Harney would have been mortally wounded if she hadn't been invited, but she hadn't expected her to accept.

'I'm not one for parties. I don't like them at all. And I don't like foreign food. I don't trust it. But your mother's been very good to me so I'll be there,

I wouldn't let her down,' she had informed Olivia with a martyred air, much to Olivia's dismay. She'd only asked her out of politeness.

'Anyway, we haven't time for place names. Everyone can fend for themselves – it's not a wedding,' Olivia decided briskly. 'We need to get home and get changed ourselves, and I've to get the girls ready.'

'Right, you're the boss,' Alison said, giving a yawn.

'Glad you know your place.' Her sister smiled as they switched out the lights and made their way downstairs.

'It's going to be wonderful to have Alison home for Christmas, isn't it?' Esther said to her husband as he pulled the curtains on the cold, dark evening and switched on the lamp. The fire was blazing up the chimney, the flames casting flickering hues on the wall. 'Sit down here beside me for a few minutes before we get dressed up to go out.' She patted the sofa.

'That's the best invitation I've had all day.' Liam smiled at her, and she cuddled in against his shoulder and slid her arm around him.

'How lucky are we?' she murmured, content in the circle of his arms.

'Very,' he agreed. 'Wasn't it a great surprise the girls had planned for us? I couldn't believe my eyes when I saw Alison.'

'I know. You could have knocked me down with a feather. It was one of the happiest moments of my life having us all together this morning. I'm really looking forward to our meal. I hope Alison won't be too tired.'

'Well, Olivia was very firm about getting her home to bed.' Liam rubbed his thumb gently across the back of Esther's hand, where she'd scratched it on a rose bush doing some gardening earlier.

'Will you be very firm about getting *me* home to bed?' Esther teased, her eyes dancing in the firelight.

'There's no hope for you, Esther Dunwoody.' Liam gave a hearty laugh, but he lowered his head and kissed his beloved wife soundly.

'My goodness, ladies, what cool-looking clothes. Very SJP, Kate. Love the puffball skirt, Lia,' Alison approved, as the twins appeared at her bedroom door all dressed and ready to go, awaiting the promised lipstick.

'Just a light touch,' Olivia warned, her damp hair sticking up as she stood on the landing in her bra and pants ironing a pair of black trousers.

'I'll do that for you – go and put your make-up on and dry your hair,' Alison offered. Her sister was flushed and harassed-looking, having bathed the girls and washed and blow-dried their hair.

'Oh thanks, Ali. It's typical – I'm never organized to go out, and end up slapping make-up on to my red face because I've been rushing,' Olivia moaned.

'Look, stop panicking, you go and pick up the parents. I'll go with the girls to the restaurant, and Michael can go and pick up Uncle Leo while the ladies here' – she winked at her nieces – 'and I do the meet and greet—'

'What's that?' asked Kate, whirling around in her purple flared skirt, which she wore over black leggings.

'We meet the guests and greet them and thank them for coming,' Alison explained.

'Who are the guests?' Her niece looked perplexed.

'We're having a surprise party for Gran. We all have to shout "Surprise! Surprise!" when she comes in,' Alison explained, enjoying the look of delight and excitement on their faces.

'Deadly,' enthused Kate.

'Do we have to shake hands?' Lia asked, not sure if meeting and greeting was as good as it sounded, and not too sure about shouting 'Surprise! Surprise!' She was easily mortified compared to her more outgoing sisters.

'No, not at all,' Alison assured her. 'I'll do that.' The twins were chalk and cheese: Kate so airy-fairy and Lia so earnest and serious, although she had a great sense of humour and the most delightful giggle.

'Cam I, emm . . . cam I do the thing too?' Ellie asked anxiously, having just trotted into the room in her finery, eyes like saucers, and determined not to be left out.

'You can of course, sweetheart. Now let me iron your mom's trousers and then I'll put on your lipstick and off we go.' Alison was enjoying herself immensely. Her nieces were at a fun age, and she loved that they had become more grown-up and were so into fashion, clothes and make-up.

But Olivia was right about the lack of free time, Alison reflected. Her sister never seemed to get a minute to herself. It was constantly, 'Mom, can I do this?' 'Mom, can I have that?' 'Mom, will you fix this for me?' 'Mom, she won't give me my Nintendo.' It was never-ending. What a pity she had to count her pennies, Alison thought regretfully. It would have been lovely to treat her sister to a spa day somewhere. Maybe she'd get her a facial in a beauty salon in Malahide or Skerries, she decided, running the iron over Olivia's trousers.

Alison yawned as tiredness and jet lag smote her. She'd gone to bed around eleven, and fallen into a deep sleep in the lovely warm bed that her sister had so thoughtfully heated with the electric blanket. Olivia had woken her at two thirty and given her lunch, and then they'd gathered the greenery, holly and ivy that Michael had cut for them, collected the flowers from the florist and gone to the restaurant, where Alison had spent an hour and a half decorating the room after sending Olivia off to get the candles and ribbons.

Her head felt cotton-wool light from jet lag, so she took another gulp of the hot, strong coffee Michael had made for her. She should have come home a day earlier than the party, but when she'd booked the ticket in September she'd had a job and was reluctant to be away from work too long. What good had it done her ... none? Jobless and jet-lagged and worrying about money on the night of her mother's surprise seventieth-birthday party. Who would ever have thought it? If the family only knew, what a shock they'd all get. She just couldn't bear to let them know of her failure, Alison thought glumly, half dreading meeting the relatives, knowing that she'd have to bluff and lie her way through the night. It was difficult keeping up the façade, much harder than she'd imagined. She longed to tell the family of her troubles, but the timing was disastrous and her pride was more of a problem than she cared to admit.

She'd always liked being looked up to as the family success story. She liked the admiring glances she'd got as she walked down the village when she was home on holidays with Melora, when the neighbours stopped to ask her how she was getting on in 'the Big Apple'. It was hard to let go of that. Was that an indication of mega-immaturity? Alison wondered ruefully.

'Now cam we have our lipstick?' Ellie looked up at her, her big blue eyes shining with anticipation, interrupting Alison's moment of introspection.

' "*Please!*" Don't forget to say "please",' called Olivia, who was applying her make-up before drying her hair.

'*Please* cam we?' Ellie said in exasperation. Alison hid a smile.

'Right, youngest first,' she said firmly, having copped on to the fact that a note of authority worked wonders.

Ten minutes later the Hammond ladies marched downstairs, with Alison taking up the rear. 'Is my harem ready then?' Michael came out into the hall. Alison liked her brother-in-law, a jovial, calm, kind-hearted man who was the perfect foil for her sister's more uptight, edgy personality.

'OK, I'm off to pick up Mam and Dad. I'll delay as long as I can. I've told everyone to be on time, so have them all in the room and I'll send you a text when I'm leaving.' Olivia gave her last-minute instructions. 'And girls, remember your manners at the table, and no fighting and just one fizzy drink!' she warned.

'Oh my God!' whispered Alison behind her. 'You sound just like Mam when we were young.'

'I know. It's awful – no need to rub it in,' Olivia hissed back, and they started to giggle as they walked out into the dark, cold night.

★   ★   ★

Leo Hammond fastened his best braces, put on his good navy jacket, made sure he had his glasses in case he needed them, and picked up his walking stick. Old age was the most challenging age of all, he thought wearily as he sat on the end of his bed to catch his breath after his exertions. And now it was time to do something that would make his life easier, and would give him a lot of satisfaction at the same time. He was looking forward to Esther's party. It was the ideal place to make his announcement, and some people were going to get a right shock for themselves. Yes, indeed – the cat would be set among the pigeons tonight, and the village gossips would have plenty to talk about tomorrow. His brother, Bert, and sister-in-law, Tessa, wouldn't be too happy, nor would those lazy lumps, his nephews. What was the old saying about assuming making an ass of u and me? Leo's eyes twinkled with anticipation as he hauled himself off the bed and went downstairs to wait for his lift. There'd be a few asses at the party tonight, but he wouldn't be one of them!

Chapter 11

'Hello, Mrs Dunwoody, welcome. We give you nice small room for family upstairs, for your birthday.' The petite, dark-haired Chinese manageress greeted Esther, Liam and Olivia at the door of the restaurant as Esther went to walk into the dining area.

'Oh, that's very kind of you,' Esther exclaimed. 'How lovely to just be with the family. My daughter's home from America, you know. It was a complete surprise, Mai Linn.'

'Yes, yes, we know, she upstairs with little girls. Follow me, please.' Mai Linn led the way.

'Did you know about this?' Esther turned to Olivia.

'Not at all. I didn't even know there was a small private room upstairs. I know there's a function room.' Olivia pretended innocence.

'I hope Leo didn't find the stairs too taxing, he's getting very stiff, God love him,' Esther remarked as she walked ahead of her daughter. She was starving, and really looking forward to her meal.

'This way, this way.' The manageress indicated a room with a double door.

She pushed the doors open and a loud 'SURPRISE! SURPRISE!' erupted from the waiting guests. Esther nearly got lockjaw with shock as she stood, open-mouthed, as family, friends and neighbours burst into a roof-lifting rendition of 'Happy Birthday'.

'I'll kill the pair of you,' she said, half laughing, half crying as Olivia put her arm around her and Alison handed her a glass of champagne.

'And were you in on this?' She turned to her husband.

'Guilty as charged.' He grinned. 'But thank God the night's finally arrived. I don't know how many times I've nearly let it slip.'

'So that was why you were telling me to wear this dress, letting on it's your favourite.' She patted the elegant, ruby dress with the ruched bodice that fell in graceful folds over her hips to mid-calf.

'It *is* my favourite, and you look beautiful,' he murmured, and Esther felt a warm little glow at his compliment because, although she loved him dearly, compliments were not his forte.

She was immediately surrounded by friends, relations and neighbours kissing her and handing her presents. Even Mrs Harney came up and gave her a peck on the cheek and handed her a bottle of champagne. 'To drink with your daughters, because they're good girls and lucky to have you,' the old woman said with great sincerity. 'But I might leave after the meal, if you don't mind, because I wouldn't be into dancing now or anything like that.'

'You leave whenever you want, Mrs Harney, and thank you so much for coming,' Esther said warmly.

'Thank Olivia – 'twas she issued the invitation. She's turned into a grand neighbour herself, follying in your footsteps, Mrs Dunwoody,' her neighbour assured her. It was the height of a compliment, and Esther took it with pride. Olivia *was* a great daughter, she knew that, and the comparison was an affirmation that she had reared her well.

'Many felicitations,' Tessa Dunwoody, Esther's sister-in-law, said primly at her elbow.

'Ah, Tessa, thank you.' Esther felt a wave of relief that Olivia had had the sense to invite her aunt, uncle and cousins. If they'd been left out, there would have been a huff. Family politics could be so difficult at times. Tessa and Bert were prickly types. The sort you had to spit out your words and polish them before you uttered them.

'Howya, Esther?' Bert said sourly. And she knew it was the last place he wanted to be. He was so different to Liam and Leo. Bert felt the world owed him a living; he had a chip on his shoulder because Leo had worked the small family farm while he had gone into the car business. He'd never worked a day on the farm but had been highly disgusted when their father had said he was leaving it to Leo for all the work he'd put into it. Liam had been in perfect agreement with his dad, but Bert had carried a grudge that had got even bigger as Leo had added to the farm over the years, leaving him now with a sizeable portion of land with good farming potential. He was, by now, the wealthiest of the brothers, although you'd never know it by him, she thought fondly as she caught sight of him limping over to her to kiss her.

'You look mighty well tonight, Esther,' he bellowed. 'Ya'd never think ye were seventy.'

'Thanks,' she said, half mortified. There was no need to rub her nose in it. 'You look very smart yourself.'

'Have me best braces on.' Leo grinned as he caught sight of the children. 'There's my girlies,' he said proudly as they galloped over to him.

'On guard.' Kate danced around with someone's umbrella.

'Parry and thrust.' He struck a pose with his walking stick.

'Cam I play?' Ellie demanded, and Olivia went to intervene as Esther found herself in the middle of her book-club group, all delighted for her that Alison was home.

Later, as she sat at the top table watching everyone eating the tasty food, listening to the ebb and flow of conversation, seeing her two daughters chat to Liam and Leo and the children making pictures on the table with chopsticks, Esther sent up a prayer of thanks for her great good fortune.

When she came to blow out the candles on the big two-tiered creamy sponge, she felt almost overwhelmed with gratitude and emotion. The expression of delight on her grandchildren's faces at the sight of the lighted candles – in the shape of a seven and a nought – as they urged her to blow them out would be one of her abiding memories.

'I need your help,' she told the children, and she wasn't lying. She was so moved she could have wept as the last note of another rousing rendition of 'Happy Birthday', and 'For She's a Jolly Good Fellow' faded away.

'Blow!' everyone clamoured and she did, as Ellie, Lia and Kate whooshed great gusts of air to extinguish the candles with her.

She managed to regain her equilibrium, glad that all eyes were no longer upon her as the cake was borne away to be cut up. She took a sip of wine and looked up startled as Liam tapped his glass for silence. 'Don't go making any speeches,' she hissed.

'Take what's coming to you,' he ribbed, but Esther knew it was hard for him; he was essentially a shy man.

'Ladies and gentlemen, my daughters and myself are so pleased you could join us to celebrate my wife Esther's birthday. My wife, as you all know, is a wonderful woman – you don't need me to tell you all that,' he said to a big cheer, and Esther could feel herself blushing. Olivia and Alison were laughing at her discomfiture, knowing that she was mortified.

'A wonderful woman and a great companion and wife,' he continued, to more cheers. Liam cleared his throat and turned to her. 'Esther, you know I'm a man of few words, despite your best efforts. But there is one thing I want to say to you.' He swallowed, and a faint dusky red crept up his neck. 'I love you very much,' he said, staring into her eyes, and this time she did cry. She stood up and hid her face in his shoulder as their guests hollered loudly.

'Oh, Liam, Liam,' she whispered.

'Well, I do love you,' he whispered back, 'I'm just not good at mushy stuff. But I know how you value hearing it so I wanted to say it to you tonight.'

'Ah, Liam, I know you love me.' She wiped her eyes and kissed him, loving him more now than on the day she'd married him. Another tapping on a glass brought hush as Olivia and Alison stood together, arms around each other's waist.

'We won't embarrass you any more, Mother,' Alison said, raising her glass.

'But we just want to toast the best mother in the world,' Olivia finished, and the toast 'To Esther' rippled around the room.

Esther was just about to say her thanks when Leo got to his feet. 'I have an announcement of my own to make,' he said, turning to look at her. 'And I want to do it on your birthday, because you've been a very kind sister-in-law to me over the years, especially since my dear wife died. And Olivia and Alison are like daughters to me and the girls are the greatest gift of my old age. You all make me feel part of your family and I'm greatly indebted to you,' Leo said earnestly, and his eyes were bright with emotion as he looked from one to the other.

'I'm telling you this here and now so everyone can hear it from my own lips, and so there won't be any misunderstandings out there,' he said, sternly glancing down at Ada O'Connor, who had a propensity to gossip. 'And I don't want anyone saying I'm not compos mentis either,' he added, staring over at Bert and Tessa's table. 'I've decided to sell the farm; I've been made a very, very good offer. I'm buying one of those little bungalows in that new nursing-home place on the Sea Road, and I'm giving each of my girlies – that's Olivia, Alison, Kate, Lia and Ellie – a plot of land to build a house on if ever they want it, and I'll be giving them a bit of money to go with it as well. And that's what I'm doing, so, Esther, my birthday gift to you is to know that, in these difficult times, your children and grand-children will always have a place to come home to.'

'Oh Leo,' she protested, stunned as a wave of surprise spread around the room.

He held up his hand. 'Don't say anything now; you and Liam and your family have done more for me than you'll ever know. If it weren't for ye all, I'd never have got over poor Kitty's going. Ye took me under yer wing, and I've been there ever since. Now it's my turn,' he said firmly, and sat down.

Out of the corner of her eye, Esther could see the look of incredulous horror on Bert and Tessa's faces. Bert was slowly turning a turkey-cock red. If they walked out, they'd be the talk of the village. They were between a rock and a hard place for sure, Esther realized, as people began to clap and a few 'Good on ya, Leo's wafted across the room. Olivia and Alison looked flabbergasted.

'Are you sure, Uncle Leo?' Esther heard Olivia say. 'We love you for yourself and we don't expect anything from you—'

'That's one of the reasons you're so special to me, lassie, and those children of yours. And you'll make me very happy if you take what I give you and say no more about it.'

When Esther heard that, she knew they had to respect her brother-in-law's wishes. Standing up, she lightly tapped her own glass.

'Well, everybody,' she said. 'This has been a most eventful birthday, and a day that was full of surprises. First of all, Alison coming home this morning, secondly, this wonderful party, which Olivia so carefully and thoughtfully arranged, thirdly, and very special to me, my beloved's public declaration of love, and finally dear Leo's precious gifts to our girls. We've always considered him to be a very important part of our family and wish him well in this new chapter of his life. I think it's a wonderful idea for him to buy a bungalow with access to all the medical facilities of the nursing home. Maybe when we're eighty, in ten years' time, Liam and I will be buying the one next door to him.' That got a laugh, apart from Bert and Tessa, who looked as if they'd swallowed cyanide.

Tough, Esther thought unsympathetically. They'd never lifted a finger to help Leo, all they'd wanted was his land and money. They would shed no tears when Leo passed, but he would be truly mourned by her and his surrogate family.

'To family.' She raised her glass.

'To family,' echoed Leo, loudly clinking his glass with Kate, Lia and Ellie as Liam slipped an arm around his wife's waist and drew her close.

'Let me fall into my bed,' Alison said and gave a yawn that brought tears to her eyes as she followed her brother-in-law up the stairs. Ellie lay asleep on his shoulder. Olivia was ushering the twins into their bedroom, urging them to get undressed quickly, it was almost midnight. They'd lasted better than she had, Alison thought as she closed the bedroom door behind her, not needing any encouragement to get undressed.

Two minutes later she was snuggled down in bed. Olivia had switched on the blanket as soon as they'd come home, and the chill had gone off the sheets. What a day it had been, exhausting but deeply satisfying on one level, utterly stressful on another. Her mother had had a wonderful birthday, one she would never forget. It was worth every penny of the cost.

But she couldn't deny she had been deeply uncomfortable at the party, with everyone asking her how she was doing at work and what shows was she seeing, and how was her firm coping with the downturn.

She'd tried to be as non-committal as possible, telling them that she was home and she wanted to forget about work. Her cousins on their mother's side, admiring her Prada bag and her Christian Louboutin shoes, were exceedingly glamorous themselves. One of them, Tina, had even said that she was thinking of taking a trip to New York in the spring and was giving broad hints about staying in her apartment. Alison had nearly broken into a cold sweat. How awful it would be to have the word filter out that she was unemployed and living in a studio. She knew it was her bloody pride, and that made her feel even worse. Well, the old saying pride comes before a fall was never more true. The high-flying businesswoman had had her wings well and truly clipped.

Alison came to a decision: if she hadn't got a job in the next three months, she'd reveal all, but until then she certainly wouldn't be saying anything about it. If she got a job in the New Year, no one need ever know of the dip in her career. God bless Uncle Leo and his kindness. Who would have thought he would gift her with a plot of land? That would be a safety net for her, a comfort through these rocky times, she thought gratefully as her eyelids drooped and she fell fast asleep.

Leo sat in his favourite armchair and turned on the radio. He liked listening to the radio at night. It was company and took his mind off his aching knees. He felt quite content with himself. The surprise party had been most enjoyable. It was nice, at his age, to see family friends and neighbours at a social gathering that wasn't a funeral. Even Mrs Harney had enjoyed it and stayed longer than planned once she and Leo had got chatting. She was of his time, she remembered the war and rationing and how people had valued their food and never been so healthy. She remembered the black-out and the times before TV when neighbours played cards in each other's houses and had nights of dancing, singing and storytelling to entertain themselves. Simple times but happy times, he reflected, rubbing his aching knees. And now it was time for a new stage in his own life. Mrs Harney, surprisingly, thought he was making a very good move. 'No stairs to fall down or set your hips an' knees aching. I'd love it,' she declared. 'Someone to do your shopping on a wet day or if you were poorly. A dining room to go to if you didn't want to cook. Sure, Leo, you're set up.'

The more he thought about it, the more he agreed with her. He never used half the rooms in the house any more. The yard and garden had got too difficult to keep tidy and weed-free, it was time to let go and move on and let someone else bring life back to the place.

Making the decision to sell up and move to the bungalow had taken a load off his shoulders. He couldn't farm any more, and he didn't want his farm to go to rack and ruin. Leo had always felt that the land had been given to him to have guardianship of it. That he didn't 'own' it as such but was the caretaker of it for as long as he was able. That land had been there long before he was born and would be there long after he was gone. It was time to pass the responsibility on to someone else.

Let the land go to this young buck who had a feel for it. He wanted to specialize in market gardening, he'd told Leo. It would be good to know that the land was being taken care of and used for what it was intended. And even better to know that his lovely girls would have a nice little nest egg when he was gone.

Bert was furious; Leo had seen the expression on his brother's face when he'd made his announcement. Leo smiled, remembering the old saying: 'What you put into the lives of others comes back into your own.' Bert had never put anything into Leo's life. Leo wouldn't be putting anything back into his. Leo had spent his life working hard, being thrifty, not gambling on stocks and shares like his brother had. If Bert, Tessa and their family had been in any way brotherly and kindly to him, he would have certainly helped out and made provision for them in his will; he wasn't a mean-spirited creature. But he knew they *expected* to be left the farm so that it would be kept within the family. Leo sighed. His money was going where it should be going, to the ones who loved him and whom he loved, and that was the most important thing of all.

'Everything went well, didn't it? Mum got *such* a surprise,' Olivia remarked as she ran the iron over the last of the girls' clothes for Mass the next morning. They were in a children's Mass every Sunday, and tomorrow was a big day – 'Sharing Day', when they would bring toys to give to various charities to be distributed for Christmas. There had been a lot of agonizing and putting back and taking out of the toy press, but with a lot of pressure from her, their higher selves had eventually triumphed. Still, she'd be glad to get the toys to the altar.

'Everything went fine,' Michael agreed, pouring out bubbling-hot chocolate into two mugs. 'Leo really knows how to drop a bombshell. His timing was perfect!'

Olivia folded away the ironing board and came to join her husband at the kitchen table. 'Leo knew *exactly* what he was doing. He's a shrewd man. Bert and Tessa won't be able to contest that will and say undue pressure was put on him to make it. It was obvious we all were just as gobsmacked as Bert was.' Olivia grinned at the memory of her uncle's horror. 'Doing it in public like that was a masterstroke!'

'It's a grand start for the girls. Knowing there's always a place to come home to, to put a house on if they want to, or to sell and use the money to buy a place somewhere. He's a generous man, your uncle.'

'He's the best,' Olivia agreed fondly. 'I never expected anything like that from him.'

'We could always build a new house, in time, and rent this one out and get an income from it. Maybe you could give up work then and have a bit more time for yourself,' her husband suggested thoughtfully.

'*Ooohh!* I hadn't thought of that. We could give the girls a room each, and I could get a bigger kitchen.' Olivia's eyes lit up with anticipation.

'Oh God, what have I done?' Michael grinned good-humouredly.

'You've put me in great form,' his wife said happily. 'Come on up to bed and I'll ride you ragged!'

'What about Alison, next door?' He raised an eyebrow.

'She's dead to the world – she won't hear a thing,' Olivia assured him, hauling him to his feet. 'She'd better sleep well,' she added dryly. 'I've plans for her. She's going to do Leo's Christmas shopping for me and clean out his fridge. She can do something to earn her plot of land.'

'Don't be like that now,' her husband remonstrated, putting the cups in the sink and switching out the light.

'Oh, OK.' She made a face.

'Stop. Forget all that. You've more important things to be thinking of,' he said, as he put an arm around her shoulder and hugged her to him before bending his head to kiss her.

'It was a great night, wasn't it?' Esther rested her head against her husband's shoulder as the moon came out from behind a wisp of cloud and threw silver sparkles on to the sea. It was a full, round cheese of a moon that illuminated the night so they could see quite clearly as they sat for a few moments, snug in their parkas, in their favourite spot at the end of the garden, looking out to sea. The rain had stopped, and the stars glittered diamond-bright in the sky. The Plough above them reminded her of the small saucepan she boiled her eggs in. Five fingers from the pointers, Polaris pointed north. A cargo ship on the horizon, lights twinkling in the dark, sailed serenely by towards Dublin Port.

'Do you mind about Leo selling the farm?' Esther looked up at Liam.

'I think he's right. I know it goes out of the family, apart from the plots he left the girls in Thirty Acre Field, but if Bert and the sons got the farm it would be sold for development or something. They definitely wouldn't be farming it, and it should be farmed. It's farming land. And, besides, Leo's acknowledged how he feels about the girls and us. He didn't take us for granted.' Liam smiled at her.

'No, he never did that, God bless him,' Esther agreed. 'As long as you're happy about it, I don't mind.'

'It doesn't cost me a thought,' Liam assured her. 'And Bert can just get over himself. It was Leo's farm to do what he wanted with.'

'Well, it certainly made for an even bigger surprise than the party, and you telling me you loved me in public.' Esther chuckled. 'It was a day and night of surprises. How did you think Alison was? She's a bit edgy, isn't she?'

'Yeah, she's probably jet-lagged,' Liam agreed. 'I'd say it's not easy over there. I wouldn't be surprised if she's worried about her job too, but you know her . . . keeps it all to herself.'

'Mmm, it's unlike her to have ten days' leave at Christmas. Maybe it's unpaid or something.' Esther frowned in the moonlight. 'Well, even if it is, it's something that's meant to be. Everything happens for a reason, and she could do with a good rest. We'll make a great fuss of her. It's wonderful to have her home. I think we're going to have the best Christmas ever.'

'You know, I think you could be right,' her husband concurred as they stood up and walked back, hand in hand, into the cosy warmth of the house.

Chapter 12

'That's the stuffing done,' Esther said with satisfaction as she removed sausage meat from between her rings and rinsed her hands under the tap.

'And I've just finished the potatoes.' Olivia peeled the last two and added them to the freezer bag.

'Sprouts and carrots and celery done and dusted.' Alison gave her report.

The kitchen was warm and steamy as the pudding boiled on the hob, the rich fruit and whiskey aroma filling the house. The ham, covered in honey, mustard and cloves, was baking in the oven, and the turkey, white and plump, was outside in the big fridge waiting to be stuffed and draped in streaky rashers.

'I've never been this organized and had everything done so early.' Esther smiled at her two daughters. 'I'll be able to look at the carol service from St Patrick's.'

'Well, Mam, I would have had dinner in my house,' Olivia said as she finished bagging the potatoes and slid them into the packed fridge.

'You did Christmas last year and, besides, seeing as the family is all together' – she smiled at Alison – 'isn't it nice to have it at home with your old Ma and Pa?'

'Yes, it's lovely.' Olivia hugged her mother. 'The girls can't wait. Just as well they've gone out with Dad, they're driving me mental.'

'That's excitement.' Esther laughed. 'I remember you pair getting more hyper by the day the nearer it got to Christmas. Let's get the table set before they come back and give them a surprise,' she suggested. She had taken down her Christmas dining cloth with its sprays of holly and poinsettia leaves embroidered on the pristine white linen. She had a dozen matching starched napkins and, for the children, long glasses with a Santa on them.

Alison felt a frisson of happiness as her mother spread the tablecloth over the big rectangular table, which had been pulled out to its full length. Seeing that familiar cloth brought her back to her childhood, and she remembered the eager anticipation she and Olivia had felt when they saw the table dressed in its Christmas glory, and the big, fat red crackers waiting to be pulled.

Olivia took the canteen of cutlery from the sideboard. The 'posh' cutlery was only used for special occasions. Esther had polished it up the previous day, and it gleamed in its bed of blue velvet. Olivia placed four tablemats on each side of the table and one at the top and bottom. There would be ten for dinner: five Hammonds, Esther, Liam and Alison, Leo and Mrs Harney. Esther had invited her neighbour because her daughter was in hospital and wouldn't be doing Christmas this year.

'I just couldn't leave the poor thing in there on her own, sure the more the merrier,' she'd said to Liam, when she'd asked him would he mind.

'You're a big softie, Esther Dunwoody. Of course I don't mind. I was going to suggest it myself.'

'You're just as big a softie, mister.' She hugged him.

'We might make a match with herself and Leo,' Liam said wickedly.

'I don't think so, he was devoted to Kitty. But they get on quite well, and I'll be able to eat my dinner in peace knowing she isn't alone.' Esther had given her husband another kiss for good measure.

Alison had done a lovely festive floral arrangement for the centrepiece, and by the time the red and gold crackers and the candles were in place the room had taken on a completely different air. She had decorated the mantelpiece with holly and ivy entwined with red and white Christmas lights and, in the deepening dusk, the lights glowed, casting shadows on the wall, and the fire crackled companionably in the grate.

Alison gazed around and felt like an eight-year-old. Her life in America seemed so far removed from her. These past days with her family had been a balm to her soul, and she knew her parents were very joyful to have her home. She felt guilty for having left it so long to spend Christmas with them.

'Oh, this is lovely, pet.' Esther tucked an arm into hers. 'You did a great job – you should take up flower arranging.'

'I might.' She smiled at her mother.

'It brings me back to my childhood,' Olivia sighed, studying the Christmas cake reposing on the sideboard. There had been great excitement at the icing of it. Esther had laid a small mirror that looked like a lake on the pristine white icing, then forked up little snowdrifts against it, upon which the children had carefully placed silver balls. Santa and his sleigh perched on one of the drifts. Two little houses and trees and two little robins were dotted around, and Ellie had gazed at the cake with awe, her blue eyes wide with enchantment.

The sound of excited voices out in the hall told them that their peace and quiet was over. Kate hurtled into the dining room, followed by her sisters.

'Oh! Oh! *Deadly!!!!*' She came to a full stop.

'Cam I sit here and pull a cracker?' Ellie sat at the top of the table and reached out for one of the red and gold crackers.

'Nope, they're for tomorrow,' Olivia said firmly. Ellie pouted, and her mouth turned down in a scowl.

'Want to!' she said sulkily. ''Snot fair!'

'Now now, Santa's fairies are listening,' Esther warned. 'Come on, we have to put baby Jesus in the crib and light the candle in the porch.'

'Oh! I'd forgotten about the candle-lighting cere-mony,' Alison said with delight.

'Can I light the match?' Kate asked eagerly.

'No, we'll let Gran do it so there'll be no rows,' Olivia decreed.

'What about Grandad?' Lia piped up, always his champion.

'Grandad and I will do it together. Come on, we'll do it now,' Esther said. They hurried out to the porch, where the tall white candle reposed in an arrangement of greenery and red and white roses. Liam handed Esther the matches, and when she had struck one, he placed his hand over hers and the two of them bent down towards the wick to light the candle to guide weary travellers and welcome the Christ child into the world. It was a lovely tradition and already several candles were flickering in windows and porches around the village.

Alison caught Olivia's eye. Each knew what the other was thinking. Each sent up a word of thanks to the Almighty that their parents were alive and well and with them for another Christmas.

'Cam I blow it out?' Ellie broke the moment.

'Of course. Go on – we'll light it again.' Esther laughed. 'Your mother and aunt were exactly the same at your age. Now come on and we'll put baby

Jesus in his crib,' she encouraged when the candle had been blown out and relit.

The crib was in the front room on the bookcase. Esther had made mountains out of some books covered in black papier-mâché. Some small pieces of Christmas-tree branches and ivy gave a forest effect. The Three Wise Men and the Shepherds clustered outside the stable, which was illuminated by a small light that shone on Joseph and Mary, and on the ox and the ass standing on the straw that covered the floor. A little blue angel sat atop the stable, and a silver star dangled from the roof. It hadn't changed in over forty-five years. Esther had bought it for her and Liam's first Christmas together. And every year it sat on the bookcase in its accustomed place and, as once her two girls had gazed in delight upon it, now her grandchildren had the same expressions of enchantment as Liam lifted Ellie up to place the small figure of the baby Jesus, on his manger, into the stable.

'Baby Jesus, have a good sleep with your Mom and Dad,' she said lovingly, stroking the little figure.

'Talking of sleep, ladies, we need to be getting home. We have a lot to do in our house, and Santa will be leaving the North Pole soon,' Olivia interjected, looking at her watch. It was almost five, and baths had to be had and hair washed before the stocking-hanging ceremony.

'Please, pleezzze stay with us tonight, Auntie Alison,' Kate begged, as Lia slipped an arm around her waist and looked up at her hopefully.

'Santa will come to you in our house,' Ellie assured her.

'And what about poor Gran and Grandad? Who will stay with them?' Alison asked, loving the feeling of being so important in their lives.

'They won't mind, sure you won't, Gran?' Kate said confidently. 'They'd *want* you to have some fun,' she insisted.

'I was thinking more about my sleep,' Alison said wryly. 'What time does Santa come on Christmas Eve?'

'When we're all asleep of course, silly.' Ellie laughed at the ridiculousness of such a question.

'And what time do you get up at on Christmas morning?'

'When the toys come.'

'That's what I'd be afraid of,' Alison retorted.

'Chicken,' grinned Olivia.

'Go and enjoy Christmas Eve with the children,' Esther insisted. 'We won't mind.'

'Pleezzze,' they all urged, hanging on to her arms.

'Oh all right then.' Alison caved in. 'Just let me pack an overnight bag.'

'Yippee!'

'Yesss!'

'Cool!'

'You have me twisted around your little fingers. Three against one just isn't fair.' Alison laughed, touched by their reactions, as they all galloped upstairs ahead of her to help her pack.

'Are you bringing your very high heels for Mass?' Lia asked hopefully, planning to have a go of them when her auntie wasn't wearing them.

'I guess so.'

'An' lipstick?' Ellie demanded.

'Of course.'

'And earrings?' Kate asked, hoping to get to open the jewellery box with the little ballerina that she loved to play with when she came to visit her Gran.

'Yes, the gold crescent ones. Will you get them out of my jewellery box, please? And then wind the ballerina up and we'll watch her dance to the music.'

185

Alison knew exactly what her niece wanted. She had spent hours as a child fascinated by the whirling ballerina.

'Come on, you lot, it's getting late,' Olivia called ten minutes later.

'We better go, girls, we don't want to be caught out by Santa!' Alison made a face.

'I don't think I want that man coming into my bedroom,' Ellie said doubtfully, slipping her hand into her aunt's. 'Cam I sleep with you?'

Alison's heart sank. Ellie was inclined to take over the bed, as she'd discovered a few days previously when her youngest niece had pleaded to stay on a sleepover with her.

'We'll see what Mam says.'

'But what about your toys that Santa's going to leave?' Lia asked, shocked. 'Santa won't come into Auntie Alison's room. He only does kids . . . no offence . . .' she said hastily, not wishing to appear rude.

'I know, pet. Let's get home and get sorted and we'll see what happens,' Alison said lightly. With any luck, her niece would be asleep before hitting the pillow, she was yawning her curly little head off already.

There was much hugging and kissing in the hall as they said goodbye to Esther and Liam, promising to keep a seat for them in the church the following morning. 'Bye, Gran. Bye, Grandad. Happy Christmas,' Lia said, hugging her grandad tightly.

'Let me know that Santa's come, now won't you?' he insisted as they trooped out the door.

'We will,' they chorused, and Esther watched them leave, happy as could be that Alison was home to share their Christmas at last.

The Hammond household was a crazy house for the next two hours as baths were taken, hair was washed and dried, supper was eaten and prayers were said. At last, to Olivia's relief, it was time for her over-excited daughters to put out the carrots and milk and cookies by the fire for Santa and the reindeer, hang up the stockings and go to bed.

'Do you think three cookies is enough?'

'Well, he might be hungry.'

'Cam I have a cookie?'

'Me too?'

'Me too?'

'Girls, I'm *really* losing my patience. You've just scoffed a huge tea. Now up to bed.' Olivia couldn't hide her exasperation. She still had Christmas presents to wrap.

'Come on, before your Mom loses her cool,' Alison intervened, noting her sister's heightened colour and the spark in her eye.

'Ookkkaayy.' Lia grimaced.

'Chill, Mom,' Kate said cheekily, not actually realizing how thin the ice she was skating on was.

'Cam I—'

'BED!' Olivia said emphatically, pointing a finger up the stairs.

Alison watched as the trio hung the red stockings on the end of their bedposts. Lia neatly and exactly lined hers up parallel to the bedpost. Kate's was higgledy-piggledy, and Ellie's on the knob of the chest of drawers because she didn't want 'that man' near her bed. Alison had promised that if she woke up and was scared she could come straight in to her.

The big bedroom had three beds in a row, with a little locker between each bed. Kate's was crammed with bric-a-brac and ornaments. Lia's held her clock and book, and Ellie's had her teddy and a page and crayons. Decorated in cream and lilac, it was a cosy bedroom and, because it was Christmas and their mother had warned them that Santa wouldn't come into an untidy bedroom, it was unusually shipshape.

Watching her nieces scrambling under their duvets after kissing herself and Olivia goodnight, Alison felt a sudden emptiness as she tucked Ellie in. She was thirty-two. If she wanted children of her own and to experience a Christmas Eve such as this, she'd want to be getting a move on in finding a partner she'd like to settle down with. Jonathan had phoned to wish her a happy Christmas, with promises of a trip to Aspen in the New Year as her Christmas gift. She knew she wouldn't be going. He was not what she wanted in life. At least she'd come to that realization. Her days of non-exclusive dating were well and truly over. She remembered JJ saying emphatically, 'If I'm dating a woman, I'm dating her.' It made her smile. She wondered how he was getting on. Coming home to visit his wife's grave must be incredibly difficult. Christmas was hardly a time of joy for him, she mused as she followed Olivia downstairs.

Michael had gone to visit his parents in Drogheda, and because Olivia wasn't doing Christmas dinner, she only had to make a trifle and finish wrapping some presents.

'Crack open a bottle of wine,' she suggested. 'We might as well enjoy the peace and quiet before the storm breaks.'

'Good thinking,' Alison agreed with alacrity. She'd turned into a lush since she'd come home, and was enjoying her red wine nights immensely.

'Do you think they'll sleep?' she asked, listening to the excited chatter floating down the stairs.

'They'd better! Because I intend to.' Olivia grinned, clinking her glass with Alison's. 'Cheers.'

'Cheers yourself.'

'Are you glad to be home or are you missing Jonathan?' Olivia asked a while later as she sat on the floor wrapping Leo's presents for him.

'No, I'm not missing him,' Alison scoffed, having drunk two large glasses of wine in quick succession. Olivia was going easy as she had to do her Father Christmas duties.

'Do you love him?' Olivia looked up at her sister, surprised by her tone.

'Indeed and I don't love him. He's far too bloody selfish, and he's mean with money. He's not what I want. I had a good time with him, sure, I won't deny it, but it's not a committed relationship.'

'Oh! Would you like to have kids and a family?' Olivia probed. 'Or are you having such a perfect life just looking out for yourself that you can never see it happening?'

'Perfect life, ha! You're a hoot, Olivia. You think I have a dream life compared to yours, you're always having little digs at me, but trust me, at the moment you have it easy compared to me,' said Alison acerbically.

'I do not have digs,' Olivia said indignantly.

'You do – when I cleaned out Leo's fridge and made some comment about the amount of food past its sell-by date, you said, "Welcome to my world." You can be such a . . . a martyr, Olivia.' Resentment was boiling up inside her.

'I am *not* a martyr.' Her sister was stung. 'You've such a nerve to say that. You're just so lucky, you can swan in and swan out on a visit and you never have to worry if Mam or Dad are sick, or bring Leo to his appointments. It's just tough sometimes and I don't think you appreciate it.'

'No one asked you to stay in Port Ross,' Alison said heatedly.

'I know that, but I'm here and I mind them the best I can. What am I supposed to do . . . *ignore* them!'

Olivia's cheeks were bright red. 'You have no idea how difficult it can be sometimes, that's all I'm saying.'

'Oh I do, I get your emails,' Alison riposted nastily. 'You just love making me feel guilty, don't you, Olivia? It's always the same.' Alison exploded as the resentment that had been simmering away since she'd arrived erupted volcanically. 'You think I have this wonderful easy life—'

'Well, you *do*, you earn a fortune with your big-deal job. You've a fab apartment and you only have to worry about yourself—'

'Wrong! Wrong! *Wrong!* On every count, Olivia,' Alison retorted furiously, tongue loosened by the wine. 'For your information, Miss-Know-All-Martyr, I've been fecked out on my ear from my job; I've had to move to a studio and sublet the apartment. I took a hammering with my investments and bonuses because the firm collapsed and because of bloody Anglo and the rest of the banks here. They were supposed to be blue-chip investments. My ass. Perfect life? HA! HA! You don't have a frigging clue about my life, Olivia, so zip it. You know, I think I'll go to bed. Sometimes you can be mean and nasty and thoroughly bitchy.' Alison stood up, near to tears.

'Oh don't. *Don't!* Sorry, Ali.' Olivia was immediately contrite. 'When did you lose your job? Why didn't you tell me? This is awful!' She was horrified. 'You should have *told* me, Alison.'

'Hell, I didn't mean to let it slip. It's the wine,' Alison said miserably, all the fight gone out of her.

'That's not something you keep to yourself, Ali, that's something you tell your family, for God's sake. So that's why you've got to spend Christmas at home. How did it happen?' Olivia topped up both their glasses and sat down beside Alison on the sofa, visibly stunned at the news.

'My firm went to the wall, my boss committed suicide, we were all let go and it's impossible to get a job in the financial sector. I'm living on what's left of my savings at the moment,' Alison admitted, utterly relieved that someone knew and she didn't have to keep it to herself any more.

'Since when?'

'Weeks ago—'

'But how are you managing? I mean, the flight, Mam's present *and* you gave me a cheque for half the cost of the party?' her sister demanded, ashen at her sister's revelation.

'Don't worry, I'm not a pauper yet. I'd paid for the flight during the summer, I'd paid for the bracelet when I was let go and I had the money put by for the party. I have some savings—'

'But why didn't you say anything? Why didn't you *tell* us?' Olivia stared at her, appalled at the knowledge that her younger sister had carried such a burden alone.

'I didn't want to worry Mam and Dad. I didn't want to ruin the party. I didn't want everyone feeling sorry for me, especially Bert and Tessa and that other pair of oompa loompas. I couldn't bear their faux sympathy, because they're the type to be delighted that I've come a cropper.'

'Ah, shag them, who cares what they think?' Olivia retorted.

'I know, but it's mortifying all the same. You know, I was flying high and now I've hit rock bottom, and my pride is dented as well as my bank balance.' Alison shrugged.

'What are you going to do?'

'I can ride it out for three more months. After that I'm on my uppers, and if I don't get a job I'll probably have to come home and sponge off Mam and Dad,' said Alison flatly.

'Don't say that,' Olivia protested heatedly. 'You know they wouldn't think like that. We're family, we muck in together. Michael and I'll help you out. I'm sure Leo would too until you get on your feet again. Promise if you're absolutely stuck you'll come to me.' Olivia caught her by the hand. 'I didn't mean to be a bitch, I've got fierce PMT and, I swear to God, I'm like a briar sometimes. I don't know how Michael puts up with me,' she said shakily, as tears came to her eyes.

'Don't be daft – he loves ya.' Alison put her glass down and hugged her. 'Let's not fight,' she said.

'I'm really sorry, Ali, about everything – about whinging and moaning. If only I'd known.'

'Forget it, you've every right to moan. I know it's not easy for you. I don't know how you do it, to be honest. You're pulled in every direction. You're right, I do only have myself to think about,' Alison admitted.

'Ah, don't mind me, I was just feeling sorry for myself.' Olivia gave a teary grin.

'Right back at ya, sis.' Alison took a slug of wine and gave a rueful chuckle. 'Look at the pair of us; if Michael comes in he'll be horrified.'

'He'd go mad knowing you never told us you were in trouble,' Olivia said sombrely. 'Promise me you'll come to us if you need a helping hand.'

'I promise, honest, but don't say a word unless I tell you to. I'm not going to ruin Mam and Dad's Christmas. They're really enjoying it because we're all together.'

'I won't,' agreed Olivia. 'But no more secrets, OK?'

'OK. Look, I might be lucky and get a job. Or I can move to Europe. I've Googled up a few positions that I could apply for. Actually, there was one in Dublin that would suit, there may be more, so I'm not panicking.'

'Could you not marry that guy Jonathan and divorce him and get a hefty settlement?' Olivia arched an eyebrow at her.

Alison giggled tipsily. 'If the worst comes to the worst, I'll think about it.'

'Isn't there *anybody* you fancy?' her sister asked hopefully.

'Well, there's this guy in my building. He's Irish, he's a fine thing and we get on great, but I only found out before I came home that his wife died in a car crash four years ago, so he's off the market. He comes home at Christmas to visit his parents and go to the grave. He's going to be in Dublin in a few days' time, so we're going to link up. But he has a lot of baggage and oh . . . I don't know.' She sighed.

'A widower! Oh God it gets worse. What *are* we going to do with you?' Olivia shook her head.

'I know! Could you not have a bit of luck?'

'At least you have Leo's plot,' Olivia said, drinking more wine and cutting her Sellotape in a rather crooked line.

'A woman of property and a spinster to boot. I'd be the catch of the parish!' Alison snorted.

'Remember Tim Griffin?' Olivia said slyly. 'He said you were the finest-looking girl that ever went up to receive communion—'

'Stop it. He was a dirty auld lecher. No wonder he never got married.' Alison shuddered.

'Well, he has twenty acres adjoining Leo's land; it could be a match made in heaven,' teased Olivia. 'You could march up the aisle in your wellies, seeing as he never wears anything else.'

'Ha ha, you're hilarious!' But Alison laughed in spite of herself, glad that she didn't have to carry the burden of her secret life on her own any more. They might have their little tiffs, but she knew as sure as day turned into night that Olivia would always be there for her, and she too would always be on hand for her dearly loved sister, no matter what the future held.

Chapter 13

'He's come! He's come!' Lia was standing by Alison's bed, shaking her. Light spilled in from the landing, making her blink rapidly several times. She struggled to disorientated consciousness, from a deep sleep that was fuelled by the relief of confession and red wine. It seemed as though she had just laid her head on the pillow. 'Who . . . what . . .?'

'Santa. Santa has come.' The normally restrained Lia was almost bursting with glee, her fine, caramel hair mussed all over her head. Behind her Ellie was standing motionless, unable to speak with the thrill of it all, her eyes two big blue orbs as she stared at Alison. With her halo of golden curls she looked almost angelic.

As she sat up, she could hear Kate screeching *piercingly* next door: 'Mom, Dad, wake up, he's come.' She shook her head to clear it. At least she'd been woken with a shake – screeching would have been unendurable with the state of her head! *And you think you might want children*, she thought in wry amusement as she struggled out of bed.

'What time is it?' Olivia mumbled as she staggered on to the landing, hair sticking straight up.

'Something unearthly,' Alison assured her.

'Three thirty, not bad,' Michael called, glancing at the alarm clock beside the bed as he struggled into his dressing gown.

'Mom! Mom! I got a bike. We all got a bike!' Lia was white with tiredness and excitement.

'Mom! Mom! I got Swim To Me Puppy and Make Me Better with Rairity.'

'And me and Lia got Diddl and Diddlina—'

'Who?' Alison was highly entertained at this stage.

'Diddl and Diddlina,' Kate said patiently. 'They're brilliant!'

'Sounds faintly blue to me . . .' whispered Alison to Olivia.

'Stop it, you!' Olivia snorted, as they followed the girls into their bedroom.

'And Mom! The milk and cookies are gone, and the carrots have big teeth marks in them.' Kate glanced over her shoulder as she knelt on the floor, pulling open the packaging on her toys.

'Go way! Big ones!' Olivia glanced at Michael, who had manfully chewed two large carrots.

'Massive!'

'Don't eat too many sweets now, Ellie,' Olivia warned her youngest daughter, whose cheeks were bulging as she explored the contents of her Christmas stocking. It brought a sudden rush of memories to Alison as she sat on Ellie's bed watching the scene.

Memories of her and Olivia waking to feel the weight of something heavy against their feet. The exhilaration, tinged with a little fear. Had Santa come? Was he still in the house? The feeling of absolute magic in the air. That one very special night where anything was possible. Racing into their parents' room waving overflowing stockings. Racing back to the bedroom to explore their toys. Her favourite had been a cash register that gave a ding when the drawer opened, just like a real one, and a shop with tiny jars of sweets and pretend packets of groceries. Looking at Ellie chomping on her sweets, she remembered the thrill of being able to eat sweets in the middle of the night, knowing there'd still be more in the morning. The glee of rummaging in her sock to find shiny new coins, a satsuma, the much longed for sweets, balloons, hair slides and hair bands and a plethora of other little goodies that brought joy to their childish hearts.

It really was a cycle, she thought as she watched Michael on his knees, with Ellie unpacking her Swim To Me Puppy, and Olivia's head bent close to Lia's as they studied a beautiful book of illustrated Christmas stories.

Even though she was part of it, she felt a sudden surge of loneliness, wondering had she been right to focus so intensely on her career and let relationships fall by the wayside in her desire to climb the ladder. Olivia had once said to her that she truly felt that women couldn't have it all, career *and* motherhood, because both needed one hundred per cent attention. Watching the way her sister had juggled work and family commitments the past week, she was beginning to agree with her. She knew if she'd had children, she'd never have been able to spend any amount of decent time with them if she was working the way she'd been working in New York. She would have had to hire a nanny, like many of her colleagues did. Mothers working outside the home had a hard tread-mill to run on. Was it worth it in the end, she wondered, all the struggling and juggling? Even though her sister worked just mornings, she seemed to be always rushing around; she rarely sat down, except for an hour or two at night.

But she was making a huge success of rearing her girls. They were lively, happy, confident little beings, completely secure in life – what a high achievement was that? Alison acknowledged this as she watched Olivia completely engrossed in the Diddl and Diddlina that Kate was showing her, while Ellie had a little arm around her mother's neck pointing out some new discovery in her stocking. Michael was admiring a pair of swanky hair combs that Lia had got.

There was a lot more to life than work and wealth and high living, thought Alison ruefully. For all her hard work and all the money she'd earned and invested, and all the high living she'd done, she didn't have a huge amount to show for it. Maybe it was time for a rethink, she reflected as Ellie came and nuzzled up close to her to show her a pen with a pink fairy on top that she'd got in her stocking. Alison lifted her on to her lap and held her close as she examined the pen.

'You know, Auntie Alison, you're very good at snuggling,' her niece informed her matter-of-factly.

'Am I?' she said, rather pleased with this unexpected compliment.

'Yes, you're a very good snuggler,' Ellie said firmly, waving the twinkling fairy this way and that.

'High praise,' said Olivia, who had overheard the comment.

'It certainly is.' Alison smiled. 'I feel just as proud as the day I got my degree.'

'Right, ladies, back into bed. We have early Mass, and we don't want you yawning on the altar when you're doing your play.' Olivia hauled herself up off the floor.

'I'm bringing Swim To Me Puppy to bed,' Ellie yawned, leaning against Alison's shoulder.

'Good idea, he'd probably like a cuddle in bed,' Alison said, as she slipped the little girl under the duvet and tucked her up snug.

'Why have you no little girls?' her niece asked, in that very direct way children have.

'Er . . . ah . . . Holy God didn't give me any yet.' She managed what she thought was a perfectly reasonable explanation.

'Well, I'm going to ask him to give you some. But you need a daddy too, don't you?'

'Umm—'

'Daddy and husband are the same thing at the moment,' murmured Olivia, smirking at her sister and enjoying the discussion immensely.

'I'd guessed,' Alison said dryly. 'You say your prayers to Holy God and we'll see what happens.' She kissed Ellie lightly on the forehead. 'Go back to sleep now, pet. 'Night girls, see you in the morning.' She blew a kiss to the twins as they clambered into bed.

''Night, Auntie Alison,' they called sleepily.

'Sleep tight, don't let the bugs bite,' added Lia, blowing her a kiss back.

Smiling, Alison slid back under her duvet and burrowed into the slight hollow in the bed. This time last year she had been sipping mulled wine at a party in a snazzy penthouse in Aspen with fabulous views and she thought she was having the most fantastic Christmas. She'd felt so smug about it she'd almost felt sorry for anyone who wasn't her. And tonight,

205

she wouldn't swap where she was or whom she was with for a million dollars . . . *and* she was a very good snuggler to boot. That was an accolade she would treasure for the rest of her life. She smiled in the dark as the house became silent again, apart from the companionable creaks and groans of floorboards and pipes and a gurgling immersion that reminded her of her small studio. She wondered how JJ was getting on, knowing that he would probably visit his wife's grave on Christmas Day, while she was being cosseted and cherished by her nearest and dearest. She found herself saying a prayer for him, and she hadn't said prayers for anyone for as long as she could remember. This Christmas was bringing her back to basics in more ways than one, Alison thought drowsily as her eyes closed and she drifted into a dreamless sleep.

It was a bright, crisp, cold sunny morning as Olivia and her brood set off down the street to walk to church. Michael and Alison were tidying up. Olivia had to bring the girls to the church three-quarters of an hour early so they could change into their costumes for their nativity play. Their breath froze vapour-white in the frosty air, and Ellie was entranced, huffing and puffing her way down the path as she followed her older sisters, who were hopping and skipping like two marionettes. Olivia watched her three precious gifts and her heart lifted. How lucky she was, she reflected, to have three healthy, happy children, a good and loving husband, parents to cherish and a job to pay the bills. She'd often compared her life to Alison's and felt hers was humdrum and a tad boring even, but no more. After last night's revelation, she felt utterly sorry for her sister. Her career, in which she had invested so much time and effort, was in tatters – temporarily anyway – her best friend was on another coast, the guy she'd been dating seemed somewhat shallow, to say the least. She wouldn't want to swap places with her under any circumstances.

There was an energy around the village that was different to other days, and even though she knew it was fanciful, it was as if there were magic in the air. She saw a neighbour further along the road with her little boy going into the church grounds and she watched him skipping along like the twins and wondered what was it about children that they couldn't walk anywhere, they had to run or jump or skip.

Houses still had a sleepy look about them, blinds drawn, gates closed, cars resting in driveways. In half an hour, the village would come to life as Mass-goers in their Christmas finery made their way along the main street to the old stone church opposite White Horse Lane. The clip-clop of high heels against pavement, the giddy gaiety of excited children, neighbours calling out Christmas greetings to each other. Clusters of friends and relatives standing on the steps of the church or in the porch making plans to visit and meet up. It was always a morning unlike any other in the village, a special blessed morning.

Later, new bikes would be tried out, first-timers wobbling unsteadily with fathers offering encouragement and a steady hand under the saddle. Rollerskaters, likewise, the nervous beginners tottering and trembling along, the more experienced speeding with nonchalant ease. Then, as late afternoon and dusk encroached, silence would descend as people went home to sit at tables laden with Christmas fare, and the lights of the trees would sparkle and shine in windows, their light spilling out into the cold, dark evening. For most, it would be a good day, for many a happy one, but for the lonely, bereaved and homeless it would be hellish, a day that couldn't go by quickly enough.

Thank God she wasn't any of those poor unfortunates, she thought with sudden gratitude, following the girls around the side of the church to the small community hall where they would change. Frozen leaves crunched underfoot, a robin hopped out of the holly bush, a black cat strolled past tail high. For luck, Olivia thought, an omen for the New Year. In the distance she could hear her daughters tell their friends what Santa had brought and she was so glad they were still of an age to believe in his magic.

She went and sat in the church to wait instead of going back home. Sun streamed in through the narrow stained-glass windows and in the nooks where statues of the Sacred Heart and Our Lady and St Anthony rested. Candles lit at the first Mass burned and flickered, casting comforting shadows.

The crib, a work of art from the Ladies Club, was outstanding as always, even down to the fresh straw used for the manger. It was rumoured that Martha Walls and Louisa Kelly had had words and a falling-out over the placement of the Angel of the Lord atop the crib, one wanting it dead centre, the other at an angle. It wasn't about the actual position of the angel per se; it was more a case of uppity newcomer coming up against intransigent old-timer, and not even the season of peace and goodwill to all would temper that particular battle.

A few other mothers like herself sat dotted around the church, relishing a peaceful few moments before the festivities and all they entailed took hold. One was even asleep, head nodding on to her chest. An early start, too, thought Olivia in sympathy, longing for forty winks herself as the children arrived to practise.

'Look at the two angels on the right,' she whispered out of the side of her mouth to Alison an hour later, as the nativity play was in full swing. A silent battle was taking place between two five-year-olds in white robes and bobbing halos who were jockeying for position in the hills of Bethlehem, aka the top step of the altar. Balthazar was standing on Caspar's robe, nearly causing the startled Wise Man to choke, giving Melchior a bit of a fright. St Joseph was yawning his head off, making his beard come askew. Kate, in her role as the innkeeper, was giving it socks on the other side of the altar, shaking her head robustly and pointing in the direction of the manger at the foot of the steps.

The ten-year-old who was playing Our Lady clutched her tummy dramatically, gave a groan and was hastily instructed to get to the manger. Lia, the shepherd, pointed vigorously to the star that hung from a rafter to distract the audience as Holy Mary whisked the infant from underneath the manger and placed him in it with a deft flick of a wrist.

'Oh that it were that easy,' muttered Olivia, and Alison giggled, enjoying the goings-on immensely. Ellie, proud as Punch, was a bell ringer, as was another little girl, who promptly burst into tears when it was her star turn.

Olivia glanced over at her mother and father as they sat engrossed in the drama on the altar. Esther still had a touch of pallor from the flu, and Liam gave the odd chesty cough. Her parents were getting old. She and Alison would cook the dinner in their house, she would insist upon it. Their mother had cooked enough Christmas dinners, today she could relax and have fun with the girls and be treated like the Queen that she was.

There were squeals of delight when the Mass was over, and the girls, back in their own clothes, came into the pews to greet their grandparents. 'Come on,

Gran, come on, Grandad, you're coming back to our house for breakfast. It's in the oven cooking.' Kate kissed her grandmother soundly. They loved when their grandparents visited, and today was extra special because there were new toys to show off.

They emerged blinking out into the sunlight to the sound of laughter and lively chat, and when the neighbours had been spoken to and wished the season's greetings, they all strolled back to Olivia and Michael's house, where a feast of thick Vienna roll slathered in creamy butter and crispy sausages and rashers which had been cooking in the oven while Mass was on, was devoured, with mugs of hot, sweet tea to wash it down.

The bikes were taken out and shown off, as were the contents of the stockings and the rest of the toys, and the energy of delight and innocent pleasure was palpable. 'It's a wonderful time for children,' Esther said wistfully. 'We had so many happy Christmases with you two.'

'Well, they're still happy, just different, Mam,' Alison pointed out.

'True, and this one is all the more special because you're home.'

'Indeed it is. I don't know what you want to be going back to that place for. Sure, couldn't you get a job over here?' Leo interjected.

'It might not be so easy to get a job in this economic climate, she might be better off where she is for the time being,' Liam remarked as he drew a picture of a Christmas tree for Ellie. Olivia caught Alison's gaze and gave her the tiniest wink, and received one back in return.

Alison had just slid the tray of crisp, golden roast potatoes back in the oven when she heard her cell tinkle telling her she had a message. It must be Melora, she thought, pulling it out of the small pocket in the side of her bag. She had sent Melora, and her friends in New York, a text to wish them a Happy Christmas. She opened it and her eyes widened:

Hope ur having a good time with ur folks and taking ur naps. Will see u later in the week if ur free and u still want 2. Will ring 2 make arrangements. Have a lovely day with ur family. JJ.

How nice of him to send her a text on Christmas Day, she thought, grinning at his message. Naps, indeed – would he never let her live it down? She'd temporarily forgotten about meeting him, there'd been so much going on but, now that he'd reminded her, she was looking forward to it. How easily her life in New York had drifted from her memory, the balm of family erasing all the worry and tension she'd come home with. Even if there was only to be friendship between them, it was a friendship well worth having.

Hope ur having a peaceful day, please do ring, I'll take my nap early so I can meet u, luv Rip Van Winkle.

She texted swiftly back. She thought 'peaceful' was an appropriate word, as it was hardly a happy day for him if he had to visit his wife's grave. What a horrible, horrible thing for him to have to do, she thought sombrely, putting her phone back in her bag.

'You look a bit down – anything wrong?' asked Olivia, as she expertly carved moist white turkey breast into slices.

'Ah no, just got a text from the friend I was telling you about. The one from the West. It's kinda sad really, here are we having fun and he's been standing at a graveside.'

'That's awful. You just couldn't imagine it. How fortunate are we when you think about it?' her sister remarked.

'Very, very lucky,' agreed Alison fervently, snaffling a piece of stuffing and savouring every mouthful.

'You won't eat your dinner if you keep picking,' warned Olivia.

'Yes, Mammy,' teased Alison.

'Oh God! I *have* turned into a real mammy, haven't I? I hear myself saying things that Mam said to us, and I can't believe I'm saying them. I feel middle age galloping towards me. It's the pits.'

The sound of a pot boiling over distracted them, and they turned to see green, steamy foam erupt down the sides of a saucepan in a lava flow that spread out over the cooker.

'Those friggin' mushy peas,' Olivia cursed. And Alison laughed.

'That's not Mammy talking.'

'Just wipe it up. You're supposed to be watching them not scoffing stuffing – you're the commis chef, allegedly,' ordered Olivia.

'Yes, bossy boots,' Alison retorted, helping herself to a taste of the ham, golden with baked honey and mustard and cloves. They could hear gales of laughter coming from the sitting room and Uncle Leo booming as he called one of the girls a little scamp.

'I'm starving, Mom, when are we having our dinner?' Kate barrelled through the door.

'Five minutes. Tell everyone to go and sit down and ask Daddy to pour the wine please.'

'Din dins. Din dins. We all have to sit down. Dad do the wine,' Kate roared theatrically.

'That one is hyper, she's going to be an actress.' Olivia shook her head, amused at her darling's antics as she and Alison began to plate up the food.

'I've waited for three hundred and sixty-five days for this dinner,' Kate declared as a plate of steaming food was placed in front of her a few minutes later.

'Well, eat it up and enjoy it,' Mrs Harney said happily, red-cheeked from the glass of sherry she'd been sipping earlier.

'Because it will be another three hundred and sixty-five days before you get it again, ye little rascal,' Leo chuckled.

'Lia, will you say grace please?' Esther smiled at the granddaughter who was sitting beside her. Silence descended on the table as the little girl joined her hands, followed swiftly by her sisters. Everyone bowed their heads as she said earnestly:

> *'Bless us O God as we sit together.*
> *Bless the food we eat today.*
> *Bless the hands that made the food.*
> *Bless us O God. Amen.'*

As she finished, Kate picked up her fork and dived in like a kamikaze pilot, spearing a sliver of turkey. 'My favourite,' she enthused, much to the amusement of her grandmother.

It was a jolly meal, full of laughter and jokes, and there was great excitement when the pudding was placed on the table, steaming and wafting the most heavenly fruity aromas around.

'That's *my* pudding,' Ellie declared proudly. 'I made that one, didn't I, Gran?'

'You did, darling.'

'And ours are at home, we made them too.' Kate was not to be left out.

'And who made my one?' Leo asked.

'We all did, Uncle Leo. 'Cos we just love you,' Ellie said, matter-of-factly, and Olivia could have kissed her for the beam of pleasure her childish declaration brought to the old man's face.

'And I love you too.' He patted the back of Ellie's hand.

'You're a lucky man, Leo Dunwoody. I can't remember the last time I was told someone loved me,' Mrs Harney said a little tipsily. She had imbibed a glass of wine as well as the sherry and, being unaccustomed to alcohol, it had gone to her head somewhat.

'Well, we love you,' Kate said stoutly, ''cos Gran and Grandad wouldn't ask you for Christmas dinner if they didn't.'

'Exactly,' said Esther. 'I couldn't have put it better myself.'

'Well, isn't that just lovely. I'm very pleased to be here.' Her cheeks grew even more rosy, and she gave a delicate little burp.

'Have some pudding,' offered Liam.

'*Plum* pudding actually.' Lia was nothing if not precise.

'Plum pudding. I stand corrected,' Liam said gravely, trying not to laugh.

As she watched the exchange with amusement, Alison wondered why she'd left it so long to come home to celebrate Christmas with her family. Perhaps her years of absence helped her appreciate it all the more, she reflected as the children eagerly pulled the crackers after the pudding had been eaten and began reading the jokes.

'Where should a dressmaker build her house?' Kate read out.

'Where?' they responded.

'On the outskirts. Ah hahhha,' she guffawed.

'Tee hee hee,' tittered Mrs Harney as everyone groaned.

'My turn, my turn,' insisted Lia, planting a yellow crown on her grandfather's head. 'How do snails keep their shells shiny?'

'How?' came the long-suffering reply.

'They use snail varnish.' She creased up laughing.

'Ho ho ho,' chortled Leo. And Alison smiled, thinking he was as much a child at heart as the girls were. She watched Liam tenderly wiping brandy butter off Ellie's mouth before she pulled her cracker with him. 'Mine! Mine! Cam you read mine, Grandad?'

'Yes, let me see.' Liam put on his glasses. 'Aaa haa, they'll never guess this one. Who is the most famous married woman in America?'

'I know, I know,' Ellie said confidently, knowing her grandfather would whisper it in her ear.

'Mrs Sippy,' whispered Liam.

'Mrs Hippy,' shouted Ellie triumphantly.

'I don't know her, I'm Mrs Harney, dear.' Mrs Harney came to from the little daydream she'd been in.

'Will we have coffee?' Esther suggested, wanting to sober her neighbour up a little. It would be dreadful to send her home tipsy.

'Lovely. An Irish one?' Mrs Harney asked perkily.

Oh Lord! thought Esther in dismay.

'Do you know what's gorgeous? A Bailey's one,' Alison said dreamily. 'I'll have one of those.'

'Me too,' said Kate.

'You will in your hat. Now start clearing the table, girls. We all have to help out today,' Olivia said firmly, changing the subject, much to her mother's relief.

When the washing-up was done and the coffee made, with a hint of whiskey in Mrs Harney's, a more generous helping in Leo's, Michael's and Liam's, and Bailey's for Esther and her daughters, they gathered around the low coffee table in the sitting room and the playing cards came out, reminding Alison of another time and place recently when she'd played uproarious games of cards.

She was really looking forward to seeing JJ. Looking forward to his teasing. Looking forward to being with him far more than she'd ever looked forward to being with Jonathan, she thought in surprise. She'd hardly given her erstwhile boyfriend a thought since she'd come home. What did that say about their relationship? Not much, she conceded gloomily, wondering why she'd settled for so little. *Never again*, she vowed silently. *New Year, new job, new outlook on life.*

As she lay in bed that night, pleasantly tired after the early start and eventful day, Alison was very glad she'd stayed on for Christmas. If she'd been working, she would have flown back to New York after her mother's party and never had this time with her parents, sister and nieces. Her connection with her family was strong and firm again, she'd never let it slip the way she had. Home was where the heart was, and family was more important than any job or career could ever be. Her mother had often said when they were growing up and experiencing a blip in life that sometimes life's hard knocks were blessings in disguise. If Alison hadn't been made redundant, she'd never have been home for Christmas – a truly enjoyable Christmas at that – and neither would she have met JJ. She hoped he was looking forward to seeing her as much as she was to seeing him.

Chapter 14

What would she wear when JJ came round to pick her up? Alison wondered a few days later as she lazed in bed listening to the sea crashing against the rocks and the birds singing in the eaves of the house. She felt pleasantly lethargic. She hadn't stayed in bed this late, for three days in a row, ever. It was ten thirty; she'd practically have a day's work done in the US. She was beginning to realize just how hard she'd pushed herself. She'd worked like a Trojan. Her career had consumed her. Coming home had been the first time in *years* that her mind and body felt totally relaxed. Perhaps it was the sea air, she thought with a smile, burrowing down into her bed, unwilling to get up just yet. This time next week she'd be back in New York and her days of unaccustomed indolence would be well and truly over. She was going to get some sort of a job to keep her going until she got her career back on track.

JJ had phoned the previous day to say that he'd be in Dublin to overnight with his sister before flying back to the States. He'd asked her if she was free to meet him in the afternoon. She'd said she was, and asked where did he want to meet, and that was when he'd suggested picking her up at her parents'. It had been good to hear his voice, but they hadn't spoken for long because he kept drifting in and out of coverage. Alison stretched and yawned. She liked that he was picking her up and that he'd meet her parents. It seemed appropriate somehow. They weren't taken with Jonathan, she'd accepted that. Not that they'd said anything, but she'd known. Not that JJ was anything more than a friend, because that was how she would be introducing him. He was a friend, a real friend. And she hoped very much that he felt the same about her.

Her chinos, she decided, that's what she'd wear, dressed up with a black Donna Karan wrap-around top. Not too fancy, not too dressed down. Smart casual. If she went into top gear, he might think she was making a play for him, and that was *definitely* not the case. Because of his circumstances, it would be very much up to him to make the first move. It had to be, for both their sakes, and she was far from convinced he would ever want to change the status quo.

'Bye, Mother, see you, Dad.' JJ hugged his parents tightly. 'As soon as I have the place anyway shipshape, I'll book your tickets to come over. Should be around May – nice time to visit.'

'We'll look forward to it, son. Ring us when you get to your sister's,' his mother instructed, linking her arm in his as she walked him to his rental car.

'I will, I'm just going to meet a friend first. Now go in out of the cold, it's a wild day and it looks like rain.' He kissed her cheek, still soft and unlined despite the fact that she was seventy-two. His father stood with his arms folded, pipe stuck between his teeth. JJ knew it was cutting him up that he was leaving. He raised his hand in farewell, and his father did the same in return. No words were spoken.

He had a lump in his throat as he started the engine and rolled down the window, and waved until he drove around the bend in the narrow country road and he could see them no more. He hated parting from his folks. And he knew they'd miss him.

He had one more goodbye to make before he headed for Dublin. Half a mile down the road he came to a tidy little village. It boasted a petrol pump, supermarket, pub, school and church. He parked in the church grounds and pushed open the old wrought-iron gate that led to the small, well-kept cemetery.

JJ took a deep breath and walked along the tarmacadam path, halfway up towards the big Celtic cross at the top. He stopped at a neat, granite headstone in the shape of a scroll. His wife had loved writing poetry, and he'd thought the headstone was apt at the time. Two large pots of pansies and polyanthus bloomed vibrantly, a colourful contrast to the white polished stones. 'Just came to say goodbye, Anna. I love ya,' he murmured. 'And I hope you don't mind, I'm going to meet a woman today that I think you might like. Hope you're flying high up there.' He traced his finger across her name, *Anna Connelly*, and then he turned and walked back the way he came, a look of bleak sadness on his face.

He made good time to Dublin. Traffic was light because of the holidays, and as he crossed the Shannon at Athlone his mood lightened, as it always did as the West receded and he drove further east. Today was different. He was making an effort to leave the past behind him and try and move on with his life. He was looking forward to seeing Alison. He liked her a lot. Liked her humour. He could never be interested in a woman without a sense of humour, he knew that much about himself, he thought with a wry smile as the rain started to batter the window. He switched on his wipers and turned on Leonard Cohen, singing 'Hallelujah' the way it should be sung.

'So where did you meet this chap?' Liam asked as he poured his daughter a cup of coffee after her brunch.

'He, aah . . . I met him in my building actually.' It wasn't *exactly* a lie. 'He makes the most beautiful furniture. He's very talented with his hands.'

'And he's from the West? A country boy?' Esther cupped her hands around her coffee cup and smiled at her daughter. 'Do you fancy him?' she asked straight out.

'Mam!' Alison protested.

She's blushing, noted her mother. *She does.* 'I always thought you went for city slickers. The suits,' she said equably.

'I *don't* fancy him. He's a friend. Actually, but please don't say anything to him about it, he's . . . er . . . his wife died in a car crash four years ago, so honestly, it *is* just friendship, so don't go barking up the wrong tree,' she warned.

'Aw God love him. I'm sorry, Alison, I didn't realize.' Esther could have kicked herself.

'He comes home at Christmas to see his parents and to visit the grave. It must be hard. It's different if you can visit a grave every week or every month, I suppose you adjust at some level, but when you only get to visit once or twice a year it must make it all very raw. But I'm glad to be his friend, he's a kind person.'

'He's lucky to have you as a friend,' her father said kindly, giving her hand a squeeze.

'Your Dad and I were great friends first, before we got . . . romantic . . . weren't we, Liam? It gave us a real strong bond that's never been broken.' Esther kissed the top of her husband's head.

'And we still are the best of friends. Friendship is a great gift to give and receive. Remember that.' Liam smiled.

'And are you still seeing Jonathan?' Esther queried as she wiped the crumbs off the table.

'Nope!' Alison said firmly. 'He's in the past. I'm footloose and fancy free.'

'There's worse ways to be, pet,' her mother assured her.

'Yeah, I know that,' Alison agreed. 'I've never had a problem being on my own.'

'Don't we know it,' Esther said wryly, and gave her a hug. Alison hugged her back. She knew her mother was dreading her departure back to America.

It was just after two when a black VW Golf drew up outside the house. Alison had been keeping an eye out, and she went and opened the front door so that JJ would know he was at the right address.

'Hey, Dunwoody.' His face broke into a smile when he saw her, his eyes crinkling in that familiar way of his.

'How you doin', Connelly?'

They met halfway and hugged.

Esther, who was up in her bedroom and had seen the car pull up and heard the exchange, smiled to herself. That was more like it, she thought with satisfaction. JJ Connelly, from what she could see, was a *real* man. Not like that yoke her daughter had been gadding around with in America. She smoothed her hair, straightened her skirt and went downstairs to meet Alison's friend.

'Did you have a good trip?' Alison asked, as she led JJ into the house.

'Got here in good time? You forget that Christmas lasts so long here. Traffic was very light.'

'Yeah, I know, it's straight back to work stateside.' Alison smiled. 'It's nice – I've really relaxed.'

'Naps and all?' He smiled at her, just as Esther walked down the stairs.

'Mam, this is JJ Connelly, a friend of mine. JJ, this is my mother.'

'Hello, Mrs Dunwoody, nice to meet you.' He held out his hand and gave Esther a warm handshake.

'And you too, JJ. Come in and have a cup of tea and a bite to eat. You must be hungry after the long drive,' Esther invited.

'Ah you're grand; a cup of tea will be lovely,' he said easily.

'Come in and sit down and I'll rustle you up a little snack,' Esther ordered.

Alison laughed. 'My mother's a bossy woman. Poor JJ complains he was bossed around by his sisters.'

'I was and how,' he asserted as he followed them into the kitchen.

'Are you being bossed around by these women, son?' Liam, who had heard the exchange, held out his hand in greeting.

'Hello, Mr Dunwoody. I guess there's no escaping the creatures. Bossiness is in their genes.'

'You never said a truer word. Sit down there and make yourself at home.'

'I will so.' JJ sat down at the table and smiled at Alison.

'So this is home.'

'This is home,' she echoed.

'I didn't realize you were so near the sea.'

'Why don't you bring JJ down to the end of the garden and show him the view while I'm waiting for the kettle to boil,' Esther suggested.

'It's lovely, not as wild as Connemara, but I love it, I have it on my screensaver,' she said, glad to get him on her own for a while. She'd realized when her mother was asking her where she'd met JJ that she hadn't told him not to mention that she was unemployed.

'Your folks are very welcoming,' JJ remarked as they strolled down the garden path to the little wooden picket fence with the wooden gate that led to the top of the bank that overlooked the sea.

'They're great, I love them dearly – and it's good to have a minute on my own with you because I haven't told them I'm unemployed or that I've moved. I didn't want to have them worrying and spoil the party and Christmas for them,' she explained.

'Gottcha! Just as well you flagged it up – I might have put my two big feet in it. Didn't you tell anyone? Have you kept it bottled up the whole time?' He frowned.

'Naw, I was pissed one night and let it slip with Olivia.'

'Good! You need to share things like that,' he said sternly. 'That's what family are for, Miss!'

'Well that smacks to me of kettles and pots, if you don't mind my saying so. And who's being bossy now?' she said tartly.

JJ laughed. 'I've had no one to practise on since you left New York, woman.'

'Is that right?' She grinned at him. 'So how did Christmas go?'

'Quiet. Spent a lot of time with the family. The bossy sisters gave me a hard time, wanted to bring me shopping for clothes and everything.' He grimaced. 'I . . . um . . . went to the grave every day. It's still strange to even say it.'

'I'm sure that was hard,' she said quietly.

'Yep.' He shrugged.

'Is it getting any easier?' she ventured hesitantly.

'Grief is a strange thing,' he sighed. 'You're motoring along thinking you're on an even keel and it just smacks you in the face again and you're right back at square one. Sometimes when I'm having a good time like that night we played cards, I feel really guilty afterwards. Feel I've no business enjoying myself.' He shoved his hands in his jeans pockets and stared straight ahead at the pounding sea, his jaw taut. She could see the muscle at the side of his mouth jerking.

'Ah, JJ,' Alison exclaimed, putting a comforting hand on his back and giving it a little rub. 'I'm sure your wife would hate you to feel like that. If it were the other way around, would *you* want her to feel that way?'

'Not at all, I'd want her to be happy, want her to move on, of course I would,' he exclaimed. 'But it's hard.'

'I know,' she soothed, 'but you must apply that to yourself, because as long as you grieve for her so desperately you keep her a prisoner too and she can't move on. You must let her go free to do what she has to do now.'

'Easier said than done.' His blue eyes clouded.

'I know, but you really shouldn't add guilt to the grief you carry. That's an unnecessary burden. It's hard enough to live with what you have.'

'Thanks. I'll try and keep it in mind.' He smiled at her. 'So you believe in life after death then?' he probed.

'I do,' she said seriously. 'I feel there's much more to us than just our bodies. I read somewhere that the body is just like an overcoat the Spirit sheds when it leaves. It makes sense to me. I read a book by John O'Donohue called *Anam Cara*—'

'Ah, he loved my part of the country, Connemara. *Anam Cara*, Soul Friend. That sounds lovely.' He looked at her, as if surprised she would read a metaphysical book such as the acclaimed writer and poet's.

'I got a present of it from my mother when I was going back to America a few years ago; I think she was trying to keep me from getting too sucked into materialism and the high-flying lifestyle I was embracing at the time. I was blown away by it. I'll get you a copy. There's a part in it that deals with death specifically. It's lovely, JJ, you'd never think of death the same again when you read it, because I remember soon after I read it, my dad's sister died, and they were very close, and we held a wake for her—'

'We waked Anna, my wife, too,' he said huskily.

'It's a lovely thing to do, and in *Anam Cara* it just describes perfectly what happens to the soul and how it goes on its journey, and it will really help you to read it, it really makes you believe in the afterlife and that there is somewhere wonderful to go to,' she said earnestly.

'What does it say?' He leaned against the small gate and folded his arms.

'Well, I hope I put it OK, I won't be able to do justice to his words, but he says that it is so important to support and comfort the beloved on their journey. That being with the soul that's passing over as it makes its way to the eternal world is an incredible privilege and that one's own grief should not burden them as they pass. That can come later. He writes about the comfort of the wake, and minding, sheltering and protecting the loved one in the familiar surroundings of their own home. What consolation it gives us to have the loved one with us for those last precious hours where all the people they loved and who loved them come to pray and talk and reminisce.'

'That's what we did for Anna; we did all that,' JJ said with great conviction. 'That's *exactly* what we did and, now that you say it, it *was* very comforting to have her until the end.'

'Well then, her soul wasn't troubled because you gave her permission to continue to the next part of her journey, just as you must continue yours, now,' Alison said firmly.

'You're wasted in banking, you should be in counselling or something,' JJ said seriously. 'I've never spoken to anyone like this before about Anna and her death and death in general, or about my feelings of guilt. How do you know these things?' he demanded, staring at her.

'I don't know, my Mam is very strong about learning from every experience, and not asking why it's happening but what you're learning from it. She always maintains that when one door closes another one opens that leads to something better.'

'Is that why you're so calm about all the money you lost?' He was really curious by now.

Alison laughed. 'Trust me I wasn't *that* calm, especially at the beginning. I was freaking out. I was *so* angry. But I've seen enough of it in business to know if you let losses like that eat away at you, you become bitter and enraged and you can think of nothing else and it ruins your life. I had to come home really, to connect properly with my Mam's kind of thinking again. I was losing all that in America. So in a weird way it was a gift to me, telling me to cop on to myself. So I'm taking my hammering on the chin and smiling, or at least trying to.'

'You're doing great, Dunwoody,' he approved, his eyes full of admiration.

'You're not doing so bad yourself, Connelly,' she assured him warmly, and they smiled at each other as the bond that had been there from the beginning strengthened between them in the most comforting and comfortable way.

'Thanks. Thanks for being a pal. It was great to talk like that,' he said, with a hint of embarrassment.

'Any time, that's what friends are for,' she said lightly, not wanting to make a big deal of it for him.

'So' – he stretched as if a burden had lifted – 'would you like to go for a drink or what would you like to do?'

'We could go for a walk on the beach and then have a big mug of hot chocolate in the café in the village. It's *gorgeous*,' she suggested.

'Sounds good to me,' he agreed, and they turned to walk back to the kitchen.

'Sit down now and eat up.' Esther pointed to the table where cold cuts of meat, cheese, pickle, home-grown beetroot, and fresh homemade brown bread awaited him.

'You'd get on well with my mother.' He laughed when he saw the feast.

'You can walk it off on the beach. By the time I've finished with you you'll be a whippet,' Alison assured him.

'Fast walker, are you? We'll see who can walk the fastest,' he challenged, as he tucked into his meal. He was just finishing a slice of Esther's pudding and creamy brandy butter when his phone rang.

'Excuse me, it's one of the bossy sisters. The one I'm staying with tonight,' he said as he took the call. 'Oh! OK. I'm on my way, take it easy,' he said hastily. 'Alison, Mr and Mrs Dunwoody, I'm sorry to be so rude, my sister's gone into labour, I'm going to meet them at Our Lady of Lourdes, otherwise I won't get to see her before I go back. I hope you don't think I'm being unmannerly by eating and running.' He stood up.

Alison's heart sank. She felt gutted. She'd been looking forward to their walk and hot chocolate, and laid-back companionship, especially after what had passed between them earlier. Things *had* changed. Now there was trust and a revealing of each to the other, as well as their easy friendship. What unfortunate timing. She pasted a smile on her face and stood up from the table. 'Just drive carefully and give her our best wishes,' she said calmly, making an excellent job of hiding her disappointment. *I should have been an actress*, she thought wryly. *I could give Kate lessons*.

'She'll be fine,' Esther assured him. 'You're not being rude at all.'

'Thanks so much for the meal, Mrs Dunwoody, it was very tasty. Just as well I had it, God knows what time I'll get fed tonight.' He smiled as he shook hands with them both.

'Safe journey,' Liam said, as JJ followed Alison out of the kitchen.

'Well, I guess the walking challenge will have to wait until we're back in the States. When are you back?'

'Two days after you.'

'I'll see you in NY so,' he said as he reached the car. He gave her a bear hug. 'And, Alison . . .' He fixed her with his blue-eyed gaze.

'Yes?'

'Thanks for the talk and the advice. I really value it, I want you to know that.'

'You're welcome,' she said. 'Follow it.'

'Sure thing, Dunwoody.' He smiled at her, his eyes locking with hers intently.

Alison smiled back broadly and knew for definite that their friendship had gone to another level, and that gave her the warmest feeling. As she watched him drive away she knew that going back to New York wouldn't be half as difficult knowing that he was there. Her 'kettles and pots' barb came to mind, and she chewed the inside of her lip. It really was time she told her parents about her current situation. Both of them at different times over the holidays had asked her was everything OK at work and remarked on the length of her stay. They weren't fools; they knew something was up. Parents always did.

'I'm going to stick the kettle on, there's something I need to talk to you about,' Alison said briskly as she walked back into the kitchen.

'It's about time.' Her mother smiled at her, pulling out a chair beside her. 'Your father will put on the kettle. Now tell us what's going on, because we know something's not right.'

Alison laughed. 'You and Dad always knew when something was up . . . it's not a huge drama. It's just that I've lost my job and had to sublet the apartment and things have changed in that regard—'

'Ah, Alison, why didn't you tell us?' Esther protested as Liam laid a comforting arm around Alison's shoulder.

'I didn't want to spoil the party or Christmas, so I'm telling you now,' she said calmly.

'You're an awful girl for keeping things to yourself,' Liam said sternly.

'But getting better,' Alison grinned, hugely relieved that it was all out in the open at last.

They sat in the kitchen until long after dusk had encroached, darkening the sky, discussing her options, and that night she slept like a baby knowing that her family were there to help, whatever came her way, and JJ would be in New York when she went back.

Chapter 15

She was really going to miss Alison, Olivia thought sadly three days later as she bundled the girls into the car to bring them to stay with their grandparents while she brought Alison to the airport. Her sister had said that she didn't want the whole family there, it would be too upsetting, and Olivia felt it was the right decision. Farewells were always distressing.

'I don't want Auntie Alison to go away,' Ellie pouted.

'We don't either but she has to go to work to pay her bills,' Kate explained kindly. 'Don't be sad, baby.'

Olivia gave a wry smile at this exchange. Ten minutes ago, there'd been skin and hair flying between them over My Little Pony.

'I think she should work here,' Lia said as she began plaiting her doll's hair.

'Don't say anything about work or going away or staying or anything,' Olivia said hastily. 'And be on your best behaviour please.'

'Of course, Mother,' Kate said snootily. And Olivia almost laughed out loud at her daughter's superior tone as she started the engine and headed out the drive.

Alison's case was in the hall when they all surged in and, again, Olivia felt a huge pang of loneliness. She could hear Leo in the kitchen telling Alison she needed to put a bit more meat on her bones.

Her sister jumped up when she saw her, and Olivia knew she was anxious to go. There was no point in dragging it out. Esther was trying to appear bright and cheerful, but Olivia knew she would be in tears the minute Alison was out the door.

'Auntie, Auntie, Auntie,' Kate said dramatically, throwing herself on Alison.

'I think you should be on the stage, Miss Drama Queen,' Alison grinned, hugging her tightly. 'Right, kisses, everyone. Time to go. I'll ring as soon as I land at JFK,' she said, briskly, but Olivia knew she was only holding it together by a thread.

The hugs were tight, heartfelt, with murmured endearments, and then Olivia got behind Alison and pointed her in the direction of the hall. She knew she had to get her out. Their mother's face was crumpling, Liam and Leo's eyes were bright with tears, and Ellie was ready to bawl.

'Out, go on,' she muttered. 'I'll get the case.' She grabbed the case and followed her sister out the front door and down the path. She'd deliberately parked on the street so that Alison wouldn't see their parents in tears at the front door.

Alison was giving great gulping sobs as she got into the car.

'Sorry,' she whispered, 'sorry,' as Olivia hefted the case into the back.

'Shush, it's OK.' She was starting to cry herself. The family had crowded out the door, and Esther was leaning against Liam, holding Ellie by the hand, while Leo had his arms around the twins.

'Bye. Ring when you get there.'

'God bless, darling, and come home to us if things don't work out.'

'Safe journey.'

'See ya, Auntie Alison.'

'Come home soon, and bring more high heels.'

'An' lipstick, my bestest auntie.'

The chorus of goodbyes undid Alison completely, and she wept uncontrollably as Olivia scorched down the street with a start that would have put Jenson Button to shame on the grid.

'Oh God! This is awful!' Alison wiped her eyes and blew her nose and struggled to control herself.

'Come back home and live, why don't you?' Olivia said irritably, wiping her own eyes.

'We'll see what happens. I'll be OK when I'm there.'

'Well, we won't. We'll really miss you. I'll really miss you, Ali, it's been great having you here.'

'I think that's why I stayed away those past Christmases. It's so horrible leaving. I'd forgotten how awful it was. I'll miss you too,' she gulped.

'Let me know *exactly* what's going on with you. No secrets now, OK? I'm so glad you told the parents and I don't have to worry about letting it slip,' Olivia sniffled.

'Me too, and I'll keep you informed. Don't worry.' Alison nodded, wiping her eyes again. 'Don't come into the airport with me, just let me out at the set-down.'

'Ah, Ali,' protested Olivia.

'*Please*. It will be too hard for me. OK?'

'OK!' her sister agreed reluctantly. 'Any word of JJ's sister?' Olivia changed the subject.

'Baby boy, two hours after she got to the hospital.'

'She did well. That was a short labour.'

'It's her third. JJ's delighted it's a boy, he needs a few male allies, he said.' Alison rooted in her bag for a mint. 'Want one?'

'Thanks.' Olivia took one. 'You like him, don't you?'

Alison was silent.

'Well?'

'He's still grieving his wife. It doesn't matter whether I like him or not, even though we get on like a house on fire,' Alison said gloomily.

'Maybe he hasn't met the right person to help him move on until now,' Olivia pointed out gently.

'*Oh!* I hadn't thought of it like that.'

'Well, keep it in mind, little sis.' Olivia smiled at her.

'Yes, Olivia!' Alison saluted, and they both laughed.

'Don't get out of the car, and drive away quick, won't you?' she urged as they turned up the ramp to the set-down area a while later.

'OK!' Olivia sighed deeply as she drew to a halt.

Alison jumped out and retrieved her case from the back. 'Love ya.'

'Love you too. Safe journey,' Olivia said, struggling to stay composed.

Alison straightened her shoulders and grabbed the handle of her case, and the last Olivia saw of her was her striding through the door of Departures with her glorious auburn mane blowing in the wind. As she edged back out into the traffic, she burst into tears.

She'd seen a different side to her sister this time, a softer, more vulnerable side. And after their little tiff, Olivia finally felt Alison was more aware of her pressures, just as Olivia was now much more attuned to the pressure Alison was under. The grass on her side of the fence no longer seemed as green as Olivia had imagined it. In fact, she wouldn't want Alison's life at all, Olivia decided as she hurried weepily home to the bosom of her family.

She would not cry, Alison vowed, biting her lip hard as the great green and white jet roared down the runway and lifted its great bulk into the sky, soaring over the green fields of North County Dublin and banking steeply to head west. Leaving home today had been the hardest thing she'd ever done. Age was beginning to creep up on Esther and Liam. It was unsettling to acknowledge that they had more years behind them than ahead of them. Watching her parents, Leo and the girls waving at her from the drive had been crucifying. For the first time, she realized how greatly loved she was. For the first time, too, she realized what a balm home was to the spirit and how lucky she was. She knew many people for whom home meant misery, angst, tension and unhappiness, people who were far less fortunate than her, for whom home did not equate with love.

She'd never really valued it until this trip, she thought guiltily as the M50 wound its way through the countryside beneath them and the engines throbbed with every fibre to thrust them above the clouds and rob her of her last glimpse of Ireland. The woman who had flown home for her mother's surprise party was a far different woman to the one that was flying back to America. Her priorities had changed radically. Career was no longer the be-all and end-all of life, and that in itself was a huge shift and a huge relief. So what if she had to let the apartment go? It wasn't the disaster she'd thought previously. She'd get a job somewhere and, if she didn't before the end of the three-months sublet with the studio, she'd consider her options. And one of those options might well be coming back to Ireland, she decided as she tried to banish the memory of the chorus of goodbyes that had cut to the core of her.

She rooted in her big tote bag and took the book she'd bought in Hughes & Hughes out of its paper wrapping. *Anam Cara, Spiritual Wisdom from the Celtic World* by John O'Donohue. She rubbed the gold Celtic design with her thumb and opened it to see what message she'd get.

'*There is a unique destiny for each person. Each one of us has something to do here that can be done by no one else,*' she read.

How apt and lovely and comforting. JJ would get such comfort from the book when he read it, she knew that without the shadow of a doubt. And maybe that was one of the things she had to do, to help bring comfort to his grieving and sad spirit. She settled into her seat and began to read the flowing, lyrical words of wisdom from the mystical poet as they flew high towards his and JJ's beloved Connemara, and Alison forgot for a while the sadness of goodbyes.

'Well she's gone, and on time too.' Esther flicked off the teletext, where she'd been keeping an eye on Alison's flight.

'Don't be sad, Gran, you have us,' Kate said, dropping an arm around her shoulder.

'Yes, and she's got no little girls to play with like you have,' Ellie pointed out. 'So I've asked Holy God to give her some, and a daddy for her as well.'

'That's very, very kind of you, Ellie. You're all such good girls, I'm very lucky to have you,' Esther said, gathering Ellie up on to her lap and hugging her tightly.

''Tis time for her to get married all right, she wouldn't want to be leaving it too late. She's a fine girl, she should have no trouble getting a man.' Leo threw in his tuppenceworth. 'Is she serious about that fella she's with in America? You know the old saying: A long churning makes bad butter.'

'I think that's all off,' Esther murmured as Liam winked at her behind his brother's back.

'And what about that chap that came to see her? Is she interested in him? He's one of our own too,' Leo observed.

'You know, Leo, he might very well be the one for her. I had a feeling when I saw them together. I don't think we've seen the last of him,' Esther said thoughtfully, remembering how Alison and JJ had looked at each other in a half-shy way the day he'd come to pick her up.

'Well now, what will be will be. We'll let the good Lord look after them, and what's for them won't pass them by.' Leo reached out and gave his sister-in-law a very comforting pat on the back, as Lia took out her crayons and drew a picture of Alison in what looked suspiciously like a bridal gown.

Alison was weary and heartsore as she lugged her case through JFK and headed for the taxi rank. 'Need a lift?' a deep, familiar voice said above her left ear, and Alison looked up in shock. JJ stood, strong and solid, smiling down at her.

Her lip quivered and she dissolved into tears.

'Aaahh, don't cry, woman!' he said in dismay, putting his arms around her. She leaned against his shoulder, inhaling the musky scent of him, and bawled her eyes out.

'It was awful. The worst ever. They're getting old, JJ. It's scary, and I feel so lonely,' she hiccupped eventually, as he stoically patted her back.

'Well, that makes two of us. Come on back to my gaff and we'll have a cuppa and a chat and feel sorry for each other,' he said gently, wiping the tears off her cheeks with the back of his hand.

'Thanks so much for coming. I really wasn't expecting it. You gave me a surprise, but it's lovely to see a face from home,' she sniffed, knowing she must look an absolute sight.

'Don't give it a thought, my dear good woman,' JJ said as he took her case. 'I thought it might be rough coming back, especially under the circumstances. And with you not going back to your apartment and everything.'

'You know,' she sighed, 'I've grown quite fond of my little studio, and my upstairs neighbour too.' She slanted a glance up at him.

'Right back at ya. Come on, woman, let's get you home,' JJ said easily, as he led the way out of the airport.

'Bossy as ever,' said Alison, but she was smiling.

Epilogue

Five months later

Alison sat at her desk in Arthur Morgan & Son's investment and tax management company and gazed out at the sturdy oak tree that fringed the top of her fourth-floor window. It was a glorious early summer's afternoon. She'd just completed her first month in her new wealth-management position, and Arthur Morgan had, ten minutes ago, dropped in personally to say that he was very happy with her work and hoped that she was settling in well. He was a rotund little man with ruddy cheeks and a comb-over, but she liked him. He was fatherly towards his clients, particularly the older ones who came to him in great anxiety because of the times that they were living in. Arthur's bottom line and philosophy was that he wouldn't let a client invest in something he wouldn't let his parents invest in. He was a man of great integrity, and she respected him.

She *was* settling in well, Alison thought happily. It was a much smaller firm than her previous company, and the clients were far less wealthy. She was getting less than half the salary she'd earned previously, but she had a job and a roof over her head and, compared to many, she was very lucky and she knew it. And at least the recovery from recession had started, as Obama continued to lift hearts and spirits.

She hadn't renewed the lease on her uptown apartment. She could always find another one if the time was right, she'd decided, when she'd had to make the decision. For now, she was happy in her studio. Melora was still in LA and showed no signs of wanting to come back. Alison was going to visit her in a few weeks' time.

Losing as much as she had had given Alison a freedom of sorts. She wasn't a slave to a certain type of lifestyle any more, and that was strangely liberating. Her mother was right, the Universe *was* providing, in ways she never could have expected, but in ways that were far more conducive to her happiness. Esther had often said that what appeared to be a calamity was often a blessing in disguise. If Alison hadn't been made redundant, she'd never have met JJ. What a loss that would have been, Alison thought, smiling to herself, feeling light-hearted and happy.

Today she was leaving work early. JJ was collecting her; he was finally going to show her his new house and workshop. He'd moved out, as planned, to live in a trailer in the grounds, three months ago, when spring had come, and she missed him living in her building. But she'd got to know the other tenants, and she liked the neighbourliness compared to where she'd lived before.

She tidied up her desk, sent an email, answered another and then logged out. 'Bye, Sandra,' she called to the secretary she shared with one of the other investment managers.

'Have a good one.' Sandra waved at her from her office.

Alison took the elevator, humming to herself as it glided silently down to the carpeted foyer. Walter, the doorman, tipped his cap as he let her out. 'Enjoy your weekend,' he said kindly.

'You too, Walter, you too,' she returned cheerily, stepping out into the warm breeze. She walked to the trunk of the oak tree and leaned against it, eyes shaded as she looked along the street to see if she could see JJ's jeep. Two minutes later, he beeped her and she waved, hurrying to the edge of the sidewalk as he slowed down to pick her up.

'Hi,' she grinned at him, thrilled to see him.

'Hi, yourself,' he grinned back, his face and fore-arms tanned from working outdoors. 'There's Coke in the cooler box if you'd like some.' He pointed to the back seat, and she reached over and took a chilled bottle out of the box and drank the cold drink thirstily.

'Niiiice,' she murmured, wriggling her feet out of her high heels.

'Sit back and enjoy the ride,' he instructed, swinging left and heading for FDR. The traffic was moving well enough for a Friday, and her heart lifted several miles on as she saw the Triboro Bridge in the distance. It was nice to get off Manhattan sometimes. As they turned on to the Bruckner Expressway, the traffic slowed and JJ tapped his long fingers impatiently on the wheel. 'Only drawback, everyone else wants to get off Manhattan on a sunny Friday afternoon. I can do the trip in forty-five minutes on a normal day,' he said as he geared up again and moved a few hundred yards.

After they crossed the bridge, he took the left ramp on to I-278E and headed upstate towards New England, leaving Pelham Manor and New Rochelle behind until he took the turn-off to Larchmont on the shore of Long Island Sound.

'This is *lovely*, JJ! I've never been this far upstate. It's very New England. It's great to be so near the water, it's fabulous!' Alison enthused, eyes swivelling left and right.

'Yeah, and it's only twenty-five miles to drive, and that's coming from downtown,' he remarked as they drove through a very pretty, bustling little town with elegant Victorian buildings mingling with more contemporary ones. There were plenty of stores and restaurants, and a fine marina. It was a completely different world to the one they'd left just over an hour ago.

Ten minutes later, he took a left at a narrow, winding, tree-lined road and stopped about half a mile along, in front of a large, double-fronted, freshly painted clapboard house with a big outhouse on the left and a trailer parked to the right. Trees surrounded the grounds, and the lawn was as big as a meadow.

'*Wow!*' she exclaimed. 'So this is where you've been hiding since you left 3B.'

'Yep,' he said proudly, studying her intently. 'I wanted to put some sort of manners on it before I brought you to see it.'

'Well, you showed me pictures of it months ago, and it looks nothing like what I saw in them. You really *have* worked hard on it. I thought you were seeing someone,' she teased.

'Yeah, I was, this is her, all dressed in white,' he said with a glint in his eye, jerking a thumb in the direction of the house. He got out of the jeep and came around to open the door for her. 'So what do you think, my little *Anam Cara*?' he asked as he put an arm around her and she snuggled in to him.

'I think it's beautiful,' Alison said as they began to walk across the lush green grass towards the house. She felt *very* certain that she was coming home.

Read on for an extract from Patricia Scanlan's
latest heart-warming bestseller…

*With All
My Love*

Out now in paperback and eBook

**SIMON &
SCHUSTER**

London · New York · Sydney · Toronto · New Delhi

A CBS COMPANY

PROLOGUE

He could feel the heat of the sun streaming over him, and had a flash of vibrant memory of lying with his brother in a field of prickly golden stubble, the scent of new-cut straw filling his nostrils, the drone of the tractor fading as it drove away, towing its bounty of neat bales to the nearby farm.

As adrenalin surged through him he raised his face to the blue immensity of sky, reaching higher, higher, every muscle, ligament and fibre protesting as he strained to reach his target. His hands curved around the hard leather of the ball and Jeff felt a rush of emotions, triumph, joy, and deep satisfaction that nothing else in life could equal. Every aching bone, every second of weary exhaustion from the punishing training regime he followed was worth it for this moment.

The roar of the crowd lifted him higher. The shiny red faces of the men he soared over, a blur in the bright sunlight. If only Valerie were here to see this, he thought with a brief pang of regret as his hands tightened around his prize and he plotted the optimum trajectory towards the goalmouth. But Valerie didn't like football. She resented the time he spent training. He should be spending it with her and their young daughter, she'd say. He hated how she made him feel guilty about his passion. It took the good out of moments like this. He twisted on the downward descent, elbowing his marker in the shoulder as he tried to grab the ball from him, clearing his way to prepare his onslaught on the box.

The pain hit, gripping him like a vice, forcing the breath out of his lungs, and bringing him to his knees. The roar of the crowd faded. Surprise and shock staggered him. He crumpled to the ground and saw the blue of the sky briefly before the darkness enveloped him.

And then it seemed that only a moment had passed and brightness bathed him in a soft light as he opened his eyes and felt a wondrous sense of wellbeing. Thank God for that, Jeff thought, relieved. He felt so well, so fit, so . . . so . . . *perfect*. Perhaps he'd imagined that brief, shocking jolt of pain. Or maybe he was in hospital and they had injected him. That must be it. He had no memory of getting there, no memory of being in an ambulance. He must have been out like a light.

Had they won the match? He'd liked to have scored that goal; it would have been a beauty, one of his best, he mused, feeling utterly relaxed. Whatever they'd given him was working a treat. The light drew closer and his eyes widened . . .

Everything was going to be absolutely fine, Jeff knew as he recognized his beloved grandmother coming towards him, smiling at him as he took her outstretched hand.

CHAPTER ONE

Briony McAllister felt the glorious heat of the Mediterranean sun on her upturned face as she contemplated the cobalt sky above her and felt the tension ease out of her body, dissipating into the soft green tartan rug she was lying on. Little cotton puffs of clouds drifted over the sharp-ridged peaks of the sierras to the north, and the breeze whispered through the pine trees.

Beside her, her 4-year-old daughter, Katie, was engrossed in plaiting her Moxie Girl's hair. It was a Sunday afternoon in September and a somnolent, peaceful air pervaded the Parque Princessa Diana, a pretty park on the Costa del Sol. Katie had wanted to go there instead of the beach, the swings and modest playground being a big attraction. Thankfully, she was now happy to play with her dolls after twenty minutes of blissful soaring back and forth on the swings, and Briony was content to lie drowsily in the late afternoon sun, her novel unopened beside her.

Riviera, a small town on Spain's southern coast, was empty of tourists, who had long gone back to their jobs and mundane lives, their Costa holiday a faded summer's dream. Where once older couples and retired ex-pats would have filled the many restaurants and coffee shops, the recession had ensured that the Costa del Sol was decimated after many years of lavish boom. Briony knew full well the effects of economic collapse. She, too, should have been back behind her desk, dealing with the thousand and one queries that came with being an administrator in a busy private hospital. But life as she knew it had changed completely the day, two months previously, when the owners of the Olympus Sports clinic had called staff together and told them that due to the current economic climate and falling patient numbers, redundancies would have to be made.

Briony knew, even before it was her turn to meet with HR, that she would be one of the staff to be 'let go'. She had been last into the department, having left a similar position in a big teaching hospital the previous year to work nearer home and closer to her daughter's crèche.

Briony sighed and brushed away a mosquito that had taken a fancy to her lightly tanned flesh. The truth was that with all the cuts in her salary in the last couple of years, the prohibitive crèche fees had taken most of what was left, and now that she was redundant she and her husband, Finn, were almost no worse off with her dole money, especially without having to pay for childminding. They had decided after much discussion that for the next year, before Katie started school, Briony would be a stay-at-home mother.

It was disconcerting adjusting to her new circumstances. Strange not having to get up at the crack of dawn and wake her daughter from sleep to feed and dress her before dropping her off at the crèche, greeting the other equally stressed, bleary-eyed parents she had got to know. And then making the bumper-to-bumper commute to work, hoping that she would get a parking place and not be last in, keeping her head down like a naughty schoolgirl and not a thirty-something, self-confident, career woman and working mother. She was still a 'working' mother, she thought defensively, realizing in these last few weeks how irritating the term was to mothers who could choose to stay at home and rear their children themselves.

Why *did* she feel guilty every morning, though, when she and Katie shared cuddles in bed when Finn had left for work? It was such a treat having a leisurely breakfast and fascinating conversations with her 4-year-old. She had already missed so much of her child's development. When she'd worked in the clinic, the time they'd had together after Briony collected her from the crèche in the evenings was often ruined by teary tantrums and squabbles over bath-time and bedtime, both of them exhausted after their early start. It was all so different now, so much *fun*! But no doubt this, too, would change. It was still very new and different. She felt like she was playing truant from real life.

She was going to make the most of this unexpected blessing. It would be her gap year, Briony decided. This unemployment that had been foisted upon her would not diminish her. She would not allow herself to feel guilty that she wasn't contributing to the family income, or that she was taking money from the state. She had paid her hard-earned money week after week, in social insurance, for just this eventuality.

How she and her colleagues had complained bitterly about the previous government's atrocious handling of the economy and the 'brown envelope' mentality that pervaded every level of society from the top down, the avarice of bankers, politicians, developers and the so-called 'golden circle'. The negligence and incompetence of the so-called regulatory authorities, too, had led to the country being bankrupted and Briony and Katie's generation, and generations to come, would carry a huge burden of debt. For all the good their complaining did. Ordinary folk like them were being hammered while the people responsible were still living in their big houses, holidaying in the sun and paying outrageous sums for lavish weddings, at the expense of tax payers. Every tea-break there would be heated discussion of some new revelation of chicanery, or some new pay cut proposed, that would leave Briony and her friends despairing of how they were going to manage in the future and worry about what lay ahead for their children.

She hadn't wanted to be made redundant from her job. She had been perfectly willing to work, albeit, she conceded with hindsight, at the expense of her relationship with her daughter. But the old saying 'When one door closes another one opens' was true. Everything depended on the way you looked at things.

This time had been given to her and Katie to strengthen their bond and that was how she would view it. She no longer had money for life's luxuries; eating out was a thing of the past for them, where once they had dined out three or four times a week and not given it a second thought. Even buying books, glossy mags and make-up now required a 'Do I really need this?' debate, whereas before they would have been tossed willy-nilly into her supermarket trolley. She'd sold her Ford Focus reluctantly, trying not to cry when she'd seen it disappear down her street, and with it, the privileged life she'd taken for granted.

The upside now, thought Briony, was that she was no longer time poor. The speed on her life's treadmill had decelerated and she felt she was slowly exhaling years of stress and tension that juggling her life as a wife and mother, combined with holding down a job, had entailed.

Briony felt the knot that had been in her stomach since she had walked out of her office for the last time loosen another little bit as she lay in the sunshine, and the feelings of failure, guilt, helplessness and fear wafted away on the balmy breeze blowing across the sea from Africa, as the scent of jasmine and the chorus of birdsong sent her drifting off into drowsy slumber.

'Mom ... Mom ... I is hungry.' An indignant poke brought Briony back to wakefulness and she squinted up to see her daughter's indignant face hovering over hers. 'Can we have our picnic now?'

'Can we have our picnic now, *please*?'

'Can we have our picnic now, *pleeeease*?' Katie echoed exasperatedly and Briony managed to hide a grin as she struggled up into a sitting position and wrapped her little girl in a joyous hug.

'Let's have our feast then. I'm hungry too,' Briony smiled, nuzzling into Katie's neck. Her daughter smelled of suntan lotion and talc, and as Briony inhaled the scent of her she wished Finn was here to share their lazy Sunday afternoon.

They had spoken earlier. He was up to his eyes doing a last edit on a report he had written for his MD. He headed the export department of a large food producing company who were constantly looking for new foreign markets. He was good at his job and in the last year the company's revenue had bucked the trend as new markets in China and Brazil opened up. Ireland's booming export market was the one bright shining star on the gloomy economic horizon and Finn had never been busier.

Briony hated that he had to work so hard, but he was driven and enjoyed it. He had *urged* her to take the few weeks to help her mother settle into her new villa, despite Briony's protests that she didn't want to be away from him for too long. Had she still been working in the clinic, they would have been like ships that pass in the night. Funny how life had balanced out for them as a result of her redundancy, she mused, as she opened the picnic basket she'd brought with them and spread out the egg, and tuna salad sandwiches, and their absolute favourites, the pear and custard tartlets she'd bought from the bakery in the big Super Sol supermarket across the road. She and her mother, Valerie, had done a shop on the way from the airport the previous day and Briony still found the difference in food prices hard to believe. They had bought two huge fillets of salmon and a big bag of prawns for half the price she would have paid at home, and a bottle of Faustino was almost a third less than what she was used to paying.

The two weeks she was going to spend with her mother, helping her settle into the small beachside villa she had recently purchased, would not cost her a fortune; in fact she'd live far cheaper here than in Dublin. She watched as Katie busied herself putting sandwiches on two bright green plastic plates, revelling in this great new adventure. 'One for you, one for me,' she sang in a singsong voice, putting her juice bottle beside her Moxie Girl. Her Lalaloopsy doll, Jenny, had been left back at the villa as a punishment for some naughty deed. Katie was a very stern mother, and the dolls lived under a much stricter regime than Katie herself did, Briony thought, grinning as her daughter admonished her doll to 'sit up and eat properly and say thank you'.

Mother and daughter munched companionably on their sandwiches, Katie chattering away to her doll, sometimes singing, oblivious to all around her as she immersed herself in a scenario with her dolly that mimicked what was happening in her life right now. She had a vivid imagination and was a self-sufficient little girl who could entertain herself for hours on end. Even so, Briony longed to get pregnant again, to give her daughter a sibling. She didn't want there to be too big an age gap between her children should she be blessed with another baby.

Briony savoured the creamy egg sandwich, a hazy memory of picnics she'd had in her own childhood floating into her mind. Picnics on a golden beach under the cliff at the end of her grandparents' house. She could remember the gritty grains of sand mixing with the egg as the breeze whipped the sand around them. Sadness pricked like an unexpected wasp sting as she remembered her grandmother, Tessa. She had loved her father's mother with all the love her child's heart could muster, and she had been greatly loved in return. And then the indescribable shock of separation, of being told by Valerie that Gramma Tessa didn't want to see them any more. The grief of that bereavement equalled the pain of the loss of her dad. Briony's eyes darkened at the memory and she brushed it away, annoyed that it still had the power to wound, even after all these years. It was a long, long time ago. Looking back only brought unhappiness and pain, and what was the point of that? For all she knew, the woman could be dead. She knew nothing of her father's family now.

And yet, she had been curious when, earlier, she'd unpacked a box of photo albums and tatty brown A4 envelopes full of old photos curling at the edges. Black-and-white ones, faded Kodak colour prints, and memory cards of long-dead relatives she didn't know. Now that she had a child of her own she had become more interested in her family history; the time would come when Katie would want to know more of her family background. Valerie had always hated talking about the past and wasn't very forthcoming when Briony quizzed her, but the photos would give her an excuse to bring up the subject.

She was looking forward to sitting out on the patio over a glass of chilled wine, the comforting shushing of the sea as it feathered the beach below them in the background, and studying this tapestry of her and Valerie's lives.

She'd not been able to resist bringing one of the old-fashioned albums with her to the park. A photo of her father and mother had caught her eye. Snuggled close together, laughing, her father squinting into the camera as the sun caught him, looking so handsome and vital next to Valerie, petite and tanned, in a pretty blue sundress and making a face at whoever was taking the photo. Probably Lizzie, Valerie's best friend, and Briony's godmother.

Idly, she finished off her sandwich, took a slug of fresh orange juice and reached into her beach bag to pull out the album with its garish plastic cover of pink daisies and splashes of yellow. A torn brown A4 envelope fell out from the back flap and a pale blue envelope slid half-way out of it. She was about to put it back when she saw that it was addressed to her: *Miss Briony Harris, 12 Eldertree Road, Dublin 9.*

Eldertree Road, she noted, surprised. That was where Valerie and she had lived all those years ago when they had first moved back to Dublin before her mother had bought her own house. Who would have been writing to her there, and why had her mother never given her the letter? And why was the address written in a different pen and by a different hand from that of her name? The fine elegant cursive, written in blue ink, was neat, precise, the letters beautifully formed – script from a bygone era, she thought, studying it intently. No one wrote like that now. Why on earth were they writing to her, this person with the graceful old-fashioned writing? The address, however, was scripted in a rather untidy, less meticulous style.

She opened the thin envelope and eased out the two pages of closely written script, and for a surreal moment was sure she caught a hint of a long-remembered scent. Gramma Tessa had always worn perfume, and face cream. Briony could remember playing with the cosmetic jars on her grandmother's dressing table and Tessa daubing her face with Nivea and spraying her wrists with scent. Even to this day she could remember cuddling into her grandmother's shoulder, as Tessa sang *'Sugar and Spice and all things nice, that's what little girls are made of.'* That sweet distinctive smell that would forever remind her of a time when life was good and she was safe and happy.

'My Darling Briony,' she read as Katie hummed happily beside her, completely oblivious to her mother's mounting shock.

Slowly, shaking her head, Briony read and reread her grandmother's letter, so engrossed she hardly heard the 'Yoo-hoo!' that a slender blond-haired woman was hollering as she ran up the steps of the park.

Almost in a daze, Briony studied her mother, willowy and tanned, looking ten years younger than her fifty years as she waved at them.

'Hello, my darlings, are you enjoying your picnic?' she asked breezily, bending to kiss Katie and tracing a tender finger along her cheek.

'Valwee,' squealed Katie, throwing her arms around her.

The rush of bitterness that surged through Briony almost made her gag as she stood up.

'Having fun?' Valerie raised laughing eyes to her. The smile faded from her lips when she saw Briony's expression. 'What's wrong? Are you OK?' She straightened up and reached a hand out to touch her daughter.

'How *could* you, Mum?' Briony's voice was shaking, as was the hand that held the letter, the letter that revealed that her mother had betrayed her in the most cruelly grievous way. A letter that revealed a litany of lies, lies and more lies. A letter that showed that Valerie Harris was a heartless, selfish, cruel bitch, who was now standing in front of her pretending to be concerned.

'You make me sick,' Briony hissed, not wishing Katie to know that there was anything amiss.

Aghast at the venom in her daughter's voice, Valerie glanced at the letter in Briony's hand. Comprehension dawned. She paled under her tan.

'I can explain,' she said urgently, running her fingers through her blond bob. 'I did it for you, Briony. You must believe me. I can explain.'